Lottery Loveboat

Mel Penrose

WHISPER PUBLISHING

WHISPER PUBLISHING
www.whisperpublishing.co.uk
info@whisperpublishing.co.uk

1st Edition

Paperback ISBN: 978-1-9162752-6-3
eBook ISBN: 978-1-9162752-7-0

ACKNOWLEDGEMENTS

With sincere thanks to the following people, who helped launch *Lottery Loveboat*:

Brian Thomas for his invaluable advice, encouragement, and enthusiasm.

David Barnicoat and the Royal National Lifeboat Institution for ensuring accuracy with nautical narrative and seafaring terminology.

Alisdair Tregenza-Hall, for all matters financial.

Jeanni Grant-Nelson, art teacher and creative contributor.

P&O Cruises, whose 2016 Venice cruise provided the inspiration for the story.

Janet Truscott, for coming up with the book title.

And last, but definitely not least, the team at Whisper Publishing, especially Wendy Wilson, for helping the author make their own dreams come true!

If you enjoy *Lottery Loveboat*, the author would appreciate a quick review on Amazon, Goodreads, or your favourite book website. Reviews are vital—a few words matter.

Lottery Loveboat

PROLOGUE

Never in his life could Harold find the words to describe that moment, yet his mind captured life-changing seconds with the clarity of a video clip to download whenever he wanted to relive it. There was something wrong with the speed, though, as if things had happened in slow motion.

For the umpteenth time, Harold saw himself slip the pink ticket from his wallet and place it next to the keyboard, hypnotised by the series of random numbers on the screen matching those on his ticket. Heart thumping, chest visibly rising and falling inside his tweed jacket, he recalled a surge of body heat, sweat breaking, metallic dryness on a tongue that felt twice its normal size. Remembering that sickening feeling as the world tilted, Harold slipped into a psychedelic unreality. Here, objects, sounds, and smells distorted and heightened, while a voice in his head told him to hold on tight to the desk in front.

From miles away, he heard a shriller voice.

"Mr Pettigrew. Mr Pettigrew! Have my books come in from Camborne or have they not? I don't have all day to stand here while you daydream it away. Lord above, you look quite peculiar. Are you all right?"

With heroic effort, Harold lifted his head, pushed his horn-rimmed spectacles up his nose and squinted over the computer at one of the public library regulars. She peered at him, impatient, concerned. Swallowing hard, Harold cleared his throat, palmed the ticket into his trouser pocket, and replied in a near-normal voice.

"I'm fine, thank you, Mrs Penhaligon. Never better, in fact. Now, remind me. What was it you ordered?"

1

She may have been fresh out of college and a few weeks into journalism, but every instinct told Angie Swan she was onto something. She sensed a story that could be the scoop of her career and maybe a life-changing scenario for the chap at the heart of it all. There it was in tiny black and white print, buried among a host of pleading entries under the heading **Male Seeking** in the personal columns of the *Porthcoombe Gazette*, one of Cornwall's weekly rags.

Seasoned colleagues had warned Angie it may be some time before she got her hands on a *real* story. As the rawest trainee reporter, more likely, she'd get the mundane jobs. This was one of those jobs, scanning the personal columns in the hope she may spot something exceptional. A human-interest story, out of the ordinary. Here it was. Angie read the ad, then read again:

Cruise Companion Wanted

Would you like a free cruise?

I am a 39-year-old male planning an 18-day luxury cruise to Venice. I seek a female companion for the duration, maybe longer.

I will cover the total cost of the cruise and all related expenses.

This is a genuine opportunity.

For more details, please register your interest asap.

Text only Mailbox: 3287241

The Ultimate Blind Date. Angie envisaged the headline even before she'd put the newspaper down.

Roy Carter, her editor, had a fearsome reputation. He also had a heart condition and the need to keep stress levels down. He tempered world-weary cynicism and grumpiness in the hope he might reach retirement, which was on the horizon. As a new recruit, with a healthy regard for your survival prospects, the last thing you did was rush headlong into Carter's office, proclaiming a great scoop in the offing. You mentioned it first to Noel Williams, your supervising chief reporter or news editor, but Noel was out. Buoyed by her discovery, Angie marched down the corridor and rapped on Carter's door.

Sipping coffee in his easy chair, Harold Pettigrew reflected. Less than three months before his birthday. Wasn't life supposed to begin at 40? Taking off his spectacles, he absently scratched his chin. Until recently, in his darker moments, it seemed as if life would end before it had begun.

The cuts were the last straw. As a librarian, Harold loved his books, but now, the long-established Porthcoombe Public Library was open for only three-and-a-half days a week. Today was one of his extra days off.

He'd become a part-timer. Worse, there was talk the library could close altogether with the next round of cuts. What would he do with his life then? Until now, fate—and his education—had conspired to deny him the delights enjoyed by his contemporaries. Before starting grammar school at 11, he'd been confident as any with members of the opposite sex. He'd even held hands, cuddled, and kissed behind bushes in the park, but the boys-only school changed that. By the time he came out the other side, he was six years behind all his peers in that direction.

An average scholar, he'd passed his A-levels through sheer hard work. His domineering father, a retired Army corporal, had recognised Harold's limitations and hammered the daily mantra. *Work, son. Work-work-work.*

"Forget about girls. These are the most important years of your life, your foundation. Focus on your schoolwork and get your qualifications. Girls can wait. All the rest will follow."

Harold's autocratic father died days after suffering a massive heart attack. In hospital, during their last conversation, he'd found the strength to give Harold one last order. "Make sure you look after your mother, won't you? Don't let me down, son. Don't let *her* down. Promise me."

To the best of his ability, Harold had let no one down. He'd carried on where his father left off, given that Mum, Dorothy, had suffered a stroke a year earlier and been wheelchair bound since. A professional daily care package and Harold's round-the-clock love and attention—including attending to her in the night—ensured he kept his word to his late father. He'd sacrificed any university ambitions, opting instead to go straight into employment after success in pursuing the advert for an assistant at the local library.

This combination of circumstances meant limitations to Harold's world. Work, and life at home with an invalid mother. Even his interest in art was a hobby he could pursue at home. Now, Harold had progressed to outdoor sketching and painting, especially seascapes, taking Dorothy with him. Parking on the waterfront close to a beach, or the start of a clifftop walk, he'd transfer her from the car into the wheelchair, take his folding chair from the car boot and make himself at home with an easel, pencils, paints, and brushes. While he crafted, Dorothy read her book or drifted to sleep.

Despite her physical disability, Dorothy's wits were still sharp. Occasionally, she'd urge Harold to 'get out on your own more' to 'find yourself a girlfriend.' He'd routinely resist. At the mention of a potential date, Dorothy would give many reasons why he'd be better off not pursuing that one. To Harold, this was unmistakable code for 'please don't leave me' and he'd drop the date.

When it came, the shock was profound, inconceivable. For several days Harold couldn't take in the enormity of what had happened, close to convincing himself he'd imagined it. In reality, Harold Pettigrew had become an overnight EuroMillions jackpot winner to the tune of £123,356,201.

Harold had never seen his mother look the way she did when insisting he gave her proof, as if seeking a second opinion on his reading ability. Her eyes dilated, then shrank to slits while her mouth, at first slack with shock, closed in a firm line. Her face, usually flushed with hypertension, changed to puce, breath quickening, getting louder. She rested the ticket on her lap and raised her head, fixing Harold with a gimlet stare.

Drawing a deep breath, she spoke with precision in a tone brooking no argument. "Say nothing to nobody, Harold, and tick that no publicity box." Then in a gentler voice. "Leave this with me for now. I have an idea that could be the making of you, but it needs more thought. Let's sleep on it."

2

Nowhere was Harold happier than his workplace surrounded by and immersed in his beloved books. In 20-odd years, he'd seen immense changes—few to his liking—but had accepted he could do nothing about progress. A creeping paralysis had changed Porthcoombe Public Library into something alien. With every move away from the traditional, Harold told himself he must accept the loss of each sacred characteristic. He'd refused to let such things bother him. Until now.

Unsettled and brittle for millions of reasons today, every little thing irritated Harold's usual placid nature. Whatever happened to the traditional hallowed hush? Nowadays, libraries were about much more than books. In Harold's opinion, books were incidental alongside other services on offer. Copiers, computers, reading circles and research hubs. Even children's activity areas, Harold shuddered.

His colleagues didn't speak quietly, either among themselves or to their customers, and casual wear had long since become order of the day. To the amusement of those around him, Harold still wore a tie. With turmoil in his mind and the publicly funded heating on high, on this trying day, it made him feel constricted and was a source of additional annoyance.

Startled by a burst of tinny music coming from the bank of computers, Harold turned his head, glaring at a young man who'd propped a mobile phone under his chin while tapping at the keys. Oblivious to both Harold's indignation and the shocked delight of the rest of the library, the man offered a racy, one-sided version of last night's activities with his girlfriend. Angered, Harold turned away, stalking to the fiction section where rows of bookshelves offered him the silence he craved.

Once there was a counter in the fiction lending library where staff, with genuine interest and friendship, engaged in meaningful conversation while date-stamping loaned books or processing returns. All that had gone, replaced by a scanner with a display screen and a well for placing books. It was here that Harold focused his attention now. What he saw had him dashing over to help an elderly lady huddled over the scanner, struggling with a walking stick in one hand and two books in the other.

"I just don't understand this at all. Nothing happens when I put my card there."

"You're not supposed to lay it down flat. You hold it between top and bottom, so the red light hits it dead centre. That way it recognises your account number, then you can move to the next stage."

A puzzled look. "Pardon, dear?"

Harold explained again, this time taking the card and doing the job for her as he did every day for other people.

"Thank you so much, dear. I'm sorry. I don't understand, I'm afraid."

"I know. It can be a little daunting."

"I've been using this library for over fifty years, you know, but it's all so different now. Everything has to be done on the lines or whatever it's called."

"No, this is not online, it's just a case of tapping your instructions on the screen and—"

"Please, don't tell me it's easy. That's what they say about everything new these days. Believe me, it isn't easy at all." She lowered her voice to a whisper. "I know what's going on. They want us oldies to be gone altogether, so everything becomes automatic with computers or whatever. They won't need humans anymore. We'll be obsolete."

Harold forced a smile. "I'll let you into a secret. I feel the same as you about the way things are going. Hope I don't become obsolete."

Dejected, Harold went back to his desk. If the irritations of his working day weren't enough, he still had to contend with the all-consuming issue of the moment, and it made him sick. That morning, Dorothy had told him tonight was the night. She was ready to reveal her proposal for him and his millions.

3

Harold hoisted Dorothy from her seat, transferred her into the wheelchair, then pushed her around the side of the bungalow. Early spring sunshine and lingering evening warmth made the back lawn the preference for their chat.

Normally, they would settle in the conservatory, Dorothy's precious place, a treat to herself after her husband's death, along with the new, extended kitchen and fresh bathroom suite. For a while, it was spend-spend-spend, but not anymore. The cost of living, and Dorothy's home care package allied with the prolonged period of low-interest savings rates, had changed everything.

Dorothy loved the house. It had been her home since arriving as a young bride, and she'd resisted friends' suggestions to sell up and move to something smaller, cheaper, and more manageable. Years ago, a well-meaning adviser had persuaded Dorothy to sign up to an equity release plan to provide a steady income stream but, as income flowed, capital value reduced. At first, everything was fine, but recent figures and projections alarmed Dorothy. Harold's spectacular win could change that, enabling her to stay in her beloved home with all the comforts and professional care she wanted.

With new-found contentment and confidence, Dorothy sat back in her wheelchair gazing around the garden while Harold collected his art materials from the car to take indoors. Dorothy was grateful for all the work Harold had put into the garden, at least keeping it tidy, but now she indulged herself with plans for hiring a professional gardener.

Emerging from the bungalow, Harold concealed his shakes as he carried a tea tray. The casual tone belied his nerves. "Okay, Mum, I'm all ears."

"Go into the conservatory and fetch the large brown envelope from the little table beside my rocking chair."

On Harold's return, Dorothy removed the printout of her big idea from the envelope, and passed it to him.

"Read this."

Harold scanned what appeared to be an ad from the personal column of a newspaper:

"What on earth is this?" he stuttered.

"What it says. It's clear enough. An advert for the personal columns. There are still such things, you know."

"Yes. Nice thought, Mum, and thanks, but no thanks. Definitely not. That's not for me."

Dorothy was unmoved, but her tone was soft. "I didn't expect you to react in any other way but at least think about it."

"I don't need to think about it. The answer's no. Thank you." Harold handed the advert back and folded his arms.

"I'm not taking no for an answer, Harold. Not yet anyway. You don't have to make an instant decision, of course, but despite what you say, you won't be able to stop thinking about the idea. You might just change your mind."

"Shan't."

"You're off tomorrow. Go for one of your coastal walks. Think about your life and where you're going. This lottery win's a life-changing opportunity and a cruise would be the holiday of a lifetime. Harold, you deserve nothing less after sacrificing so much of your life for me and you may land yourself a wife."

Despairing, Harold threw his arms in the air. "Now you're trying to marry me off! Stop it. Besides, this is all a bit of a change of heart, isn't it? Whenever there's been so much as a hint of a woman in my life, you've moved mountains to put me off the idea."

Looking straight at Harold, Dorothy adopted a serious look. "Yes, but time goes by and life is short. You never know, I may like the idea of grandchildren."

Harold experienced a rare loss of emotional control. "Good grief, Mum. Haven't you controlled my life enough already?"

"I can understand your reaction. In the circumstances, I'll overlook that little outburst. In fact, you've just betrayed your true feelings. You've spent too much of your life stuck here. Surely you'd like to see a bit of the world. And I can't imagine why any man wouldn't warm to the idea of spending eighteen days on a cruise ship with female company.

There was an awkward silence as Dorothy munched on a biscuit.

"Just think about it."

"I am, and I'm thinking this is quite a change of heart. Why are you suddenly so keen to get rid of me? It doesn't add up. Something's not right."

Uneasy, Dorothy shifted in her chair, considering her words. "We've become a tad richer, plus I have something else to tell you, although that can wait. It will all make sense to you, I promise. Anyway, can't you accept that I'm proposing this for all the reasons I've given you?"

"No."

Dorothy sipped tea. "Okay. Worst-case scenario, you at least try, and if none of the applicants are to your liking, we drop the whole idea."

"Applicants?"

"What else do we call them? We'll sift through the applications, work up a shortlist and interview them here."

"Very romantic."

"What do you suggest?" Dorothy snapped.

Harold persevered. "It'll take forever to wade through applications. We'll be inundated."

"Not if we put the advert in the local paper rather than a national."

"Okay, but that could blow my anonymity. My identity's bound to get out, one way or another."

"No, it won't. There'll be safeguards in the arrangement."

"Such as?"

"Legally binding arrangements."

"Oh, God! Whatever next?"

"You agreed you wanted to keep all this private and now we can afford expensive lawyers."

"But—"

"Just stop fretting!" Dorothy all-but yelled at him.

Harold recoiled, fearing half the neighbourhood may have heard the heightened exchange.

Dorothy took advantage of his agitation. "I've thought it through. God knows, I have nothing else to do with my time, stuck in this wheelchair. Everything's mapped out for you if you want it. I'll do everything. The planning, booking, organising. All you have to do is go on the cruise, enjoy yourself and, while you're away, think about what you'll do with the rest of your money. After making me secure and comfortable for the rest of my life, of course. There'll be a penny or two left over. The weather forecast's good for tomorrow. Go for that walk and think about it."

* * *

The coast path was the place where Harold retreated whenever he wanted to reflect. That was the beauty of living in Cornwall, never too far from the sea. If you lived in a seaside town such as Porthcoombe, a short walk took you away from your troubles.

The next day found Harold high on the footpath, the sun rising, no one else in sight, vast sea and sky and the utter magnificence of the rugged coastline all around. He almost had the sea to himself. Only one ship on the far horizon—a fishing boat chugging in the middle distance—and a little yacht, its bright red sail visible a couple of miles offshore. There was scant cloud in the sky and a mere breath of wind. Peace. Alone, with only nature's sound of the vast sea below and seagulls squawking overhead.

"Just think about it," Dorothy had urged.

To his surprise, Harold conceded that regardless of any hidden motive, his mother had a point. Now and then in life, even one as sheltered as his, you had to draw breath, take stock. This was such a moment. After all, he was weeks away from his life 'beginning at 40.' The idea of a luxury cruise to Venice with a female companion, especially if she could share his love of Renaissance art, wasn't so bad. The cool freshness of the early morning took on the warmth of a Cornish spring day, the sun beaming from a now-cloudless sky, and Harold admired pink thrift, white campion, and sea holly dotted along the path.

Settling on a small area of rough turf, Harold lay back, closed his eyes against the sun and thought about his life. *What could this surprise change in his circumstances mean?* Alone and at ease, he confronted his biggest insecurity. A lifetime's shyness of women. He talked to women, had female colleagues, but he'd never had a proper relationship. The thought of a holiday with a woman he didn't know made him feel sick.

I don't have to marry her. It's just a holiday, he reasoned. It could be fun having someone to share the sights with and if they only had that in common, so what? They'd have a memorable break and move on. He would have done what Dorothy asked, then perhaps she'd leave him alone to get on with his life.

Visions of Venice's Grand Canal, the Doge's Palace, and St Mark's Basilica loaded Harold's thoughts. Worries dissolved and the prospect of foreign travel and artistic treasures filled him with a sense of excitement, the feeling he could cope with anything, even a woman companion.

Scrambling to his feet, he gazed at the measureless, sparkling expanse of blue sea and found a cargo ship out on the horizon. As an artist, he knew paintings often depicted sailing vessels representing souls departing for unknown shores. Would he be one of those souls, heading off into uncharted waters far beyond the familiarity of Porthcoombe Bay?

4

Her warm smile and cheery tone were never far away. "Hi, Harold, I am almost finished here. Mum has had breakfast and I am leaving in a moment."

Dorothy's principal carer, Croatian-born, softly spoken Aleksandra, better known as Sandy, came highly recommended by the agency. She'd impressed from the start and had forged a solid relationship with Harold's mother in four years. Intrigued by Sandy's background, of which he knew little, Harold had watched the friendship develop.

It was clear Sandy confided in Dorothy. There were dark hints of harrowing circumstances back in her homeland. Dorothy shared snippets with Harold, although he suspected his mother learned more than she said. After Dorothy, Sandy was the nearest thing to a woman in Harold's life. There'd been one fleeting moment in the early days when, feeling bold, Harold had betrayed his attraction for Sandy with a look and a few words, the closest he'd come to making a pass at a woman. Dorothy had spotted the threat and didn't need to speak. She jerked her head towards Harold, fixing him with a formidable stare. Never again had Harold repeated the action, but Dorothy, with all her controlling qualities, couldn't stop him from thinking about her.

Approaching 30, Sandy was an attractive woman—tall, long, mid-brown hair, big blue-grey eyes, and a wide generous mouth. Harold couldn't understand why she was unattached, never speaking of partners, past or present. He guessed her looks and style had earned many admirers, including him, and often thought how wonderful it would be if she were his girlfriend.

"Right, let's get down to it." Dorothy jerked Harold from his reverie.

"Can I make tea first? It's been a long walk."

"If you must."

"One for you, too?"

"Course not. Sandy's given me a potful for breakfast."

Sandy. Waiting for the kettle to boil, Harold watched her leave. As she turned to close the gate, Sandy looked back into the bungalow, straight into Harold's eyes. There was a hint of a shy smile, so it seemed. In haste, Harold pulled back—it was rude to stare—but carried on watching from the back of the kitchen. He followed the top of Sandy's lovely head, watching it disappear below the garden hedge as she climbed into her car parked in the lane. Smiling, Harold made tea, then sat in the lounge opposite Dorothy in her wheelchair.

"I've given it a lot of thought and—"

"Yes, yes, I know you have, but let's not waste time. I've booked the cruise for you." Dorothy bubbled.

"You've done what?"

"I've booked two cabins, one for you and one for A N Other. They're both in your name, for now."

"Mum—"

"Be quiet and listen, Harold."

"But we haven't started the application process for my companion yet. Not even booked the advert."

"Yes, we have. I've done that, too."

Harold sat back in his chair. "But supposing I don't want any of this?" The tone was weak.

"Oh, for Heaven's sake, don't be silly. Ever heard the term holiday of a lifetime? The cruise will be that for you and a great deal more besides."

A long pause. "Okay, say I go along with it. You'd better tell me what's involved, where I'm going and when. No doubt you've done the homework. I'd expect nothing less."

"The cruise starts from Southampton in two months. A taxi will pick you up here at seven in the morning and drop you off outside the Mayflower Terminal. A porter will relieve you of your luggage and next thing you know you'll be outside your cabin door."

Dorothy paused, giving Harold a chance to take it all in, but he gestured for her to continue.

"You'll be on the *Gem of the Seas*, an ultra-luxurious cruiser. It's a big ship and you'll easily be lost in the crowd—no need to feel self-conscious. No one will bother about what you look like or what you get up to. The ship can take two thousand passengers and has nearly as many crew. You know the sort of thing—serving every need and all that."

Dorothy waited for a response, which didn't come.

"The ship stops at Venice, Cadiz, Valletta, Korcula, Corfu, Messina, and Gibraltar."

Silence. A bemused look on Harold's face. He reached for his tea, the cup and saucer clattering in his hand.

"Say something."

Harold took two gulps of tea. "Two months. This is all happening in two months, you say?"

"That's right."

"But I'm not sure I can get the holiday dates."

"Of course you can. You've taken no leave this year and if they say no, remember, you've won a fortune. If you have to, chuck the job. You don't need it anymore."

"Maybe not, but the library's the only thing that's meant anything to me in my adult life. I can't abandon it overnight, especially when it's facing so many challenges."

"Okay, let's deal with that when we come to it."

"And what about my companion, whoever she may be?"

"As you said, we'll have loads of applications. There's bound to be someone among that lot. I'd say a few who'll be able to make those dates."

"You have it all sorted, don't you?"

"Oh, yes, and more, but that'll do for now. Next step, let's see what comes in, whittle down to a shortlist then bring them in for interview."

5

Editor Roy Carter snapped at Angie's breathless blurting. "Slow down."

From the edge of her seat, she gave first thoughts on how she'd respond to her discovery. Carter sipped. Rushing to his office, Angie realised she'd improve her chances of an audience with her ultimate boss if she included him in the coffee round. It worked. She'd handed the hot drink, then the newspaper opened at the personal page, the male seeking advert penned in a big circle.

"I've seen some strange personal ads in my time, but this one is a first," Carter agreed.

"I reckon he could have won the lottery," Angie suggested.

"Steady. Let's not run away with ourselves."

"No, I'm being serious. There are rumours of a big lottery winner in Cornwall."

"Yes, I'll grant you that, but it's still stretching things. It's likely the guy wants to remain anonymous. I understand only fifteen per cent of winners opt for publicity."

Carter couldn't put Angie off. "All the better if we can be the newspaper to find him, get his story, and reveal his identity. An exclusive, with a headline like 'a love life on the ocean wave.'"

Carter's eyes closed. Shoulders sank, deep breath. "You're running away with yourself. Leave the clever stuff to us, eh?"

But Angie remained bright-eyed, still on the edge of her seat. "Okay, how about 'my ultimate blind date'?"

Carter's eyes rose to the ceiling. "Oh, what the hell. Yes, that's better. Nice idea, but this is taking an awful lot for granted, isn't it? Let's assume this guy is against publicity. From shedloads of applicants, how will you, as a local reporter, be his choice to accompany him on this cruise?"

Angie smiled. "I'll think of something. A different identity and come up with a unique cover story."

"Now hang on a minute. I'm not sure we want to get involved in anything underhand. That could land us in all sorts of trouble. Besides, you can't change your name because you'll need it for your passport and so on."

"I know, but that's no problem. Give me my first byline after the cruise. Keep my name out of the paper. I've just arrived in the area from up north, hardly know anyone, and the chances of this guy recognising me as a reporter are slim. I'll have a strong cover story and think of a special way to get his attention in the application process."

"I'll need persuading. False pretences, underhand tactics, and all that. I'm not sure. A colleague of mine used to say you can find enough trouble in life without looking for it."

"But you have to agree there's potential for a great story here?"

Carter's face dropped, his voice stern. "I don't have to agree anything with you, but we'll worry about that if and when."

"So, you're happy for me to respond to the ad and register my interest?"

"Seems that way, but one step at a time. Let's see where you get with that, and for now, I don't want to know about any cover story you come up with that gains access by deception. Clear?"

"Yes, but I'll have to keep you informed of developments."

"I repeat, one step at a time. If you get anywhere, I'm thinking of a compromise. You could go on the cruise, but in your own time, taking it as advance holiday entitlement. I know you've only been here a few weeks, but I'm prepared to agree to that if there's a chance of an exclusive. If you don't get the story, you've had a holiday that hasn't cost us a penny, according to this advert."

"Thanks so much." Angie got up to leave.

Still not matching Angie's smiles, Carter said. "Let's say you manage to be his cruise companion and grab a story, but he insists on remaining anonymous. How will you change his mind?"

"I'll think of ways to do that too." Angie grinned.

"Shouldn't have asked. Now that I definitely won't want to know."

6

Angie Swan sat opposite Harold and Dorothy, her application on the table between them.

While meeting the requirement of being in writing, the top page was a mock book cover titled *My Dream Cruise—A Personal Pictorial Record* by Angie Swan. As silence remained, Angie wondered if she'd been too creative in her desire to be the standout candidate.

Dorothy tapped Angie's application. "You captured our attention with this. It got you here, made you jump out from the rest, so, well done. Now, tell us more about your background and what this book of yours is all about."

Unnerved by Dorothy's candour and desperate not to sound rehearsed, Angie cleared her throat. "I came on holiday to Porthcoombe with my parents and fell in love with the place. Both parents are dead now. Dad died last year. He was a wedding photographer in Manchester, where I've spent most of my life."

Angie paused and licked her lips. As no-one seemed inclined to say anything, she continued, more confident now. "Since childhood, I've been a keen photographer, thanks to Dad. As I grew up, I helped him, got a feel for the business. Now, I want to start up on my own here."

"As a wedding photographer?" Harold asked.

"Not exactly, at least not in the conventional sense. I want to specialise, do something different from all the rest."

"What have you got in mind? There are several talented photographers out there, no doubt all offering something *special*. Falmouth University is spewing out loads more every year." Dorothy's tone was direct.

Angie lowered her voice. "I haven't launched yet. Please, don't mention this to anyone else."

Dorothy and Harold both shook their heads.

"I have an idea for a business. Golden Replay Pictorials."

"Good name. Go on," Dorothy said.

"I'll take pictures of any special event—anything at all, not just weddings—and turn them into book form."

Harold's eyebrows shot up at the word book.

"Hardback, real top-quality print. More of a keepsake than a standard photo album. Who wants treasured memories locked away in digital form? If there's one thing Dad was sure of, there's still a place for prints."

Harold was puzzled. "You'd only be printing a small number. Wouldn't that be expensive?"

"Not at all. Forget about conventional printing. You can do everything online now, which has driven the price down. Print on demand—as many or as few books as you want. Even just one for that special person."

Harold was sure he'd blushed when Angie uttered that last sentence. She'd looked straight at him. He was grateful for his mother's next question.

"How does this link into the cruise? Explain what you have in mind."

"I'll record the cruise, then produce a commemorative book just as that mock cover suggests. With your name on it, Harold."

"I'd be a guinea pig for you." Harold's response was wry.

"In business terms, it's a bench test before I launch Golden Replay for real. You know the sort of thing, find any weaknesses, iron out flaws. I get invaluable experience; you get a free book."

Harold pursed his lips and made a gesture with his hands, which Angie interpreted as no problem. Dorothy's face remained inscrutable.

"You say a book, but it would just be pictures," Harold said.

"There's no reason why you can't have expanded text if you want. It'll be *your* book, exactly as you want it to be, and, if you like, I can help with the prose. I'm quite good at writing."

Maintaining her blank stare, Dorothy placed her chin on tented fingers.

"I like the sound of it," Harold enthused, offering Angie a warm smile.

For the first time since she'd arrived, Harold allowed himself a proper look at her. He liked the tailored trousers and matching jacket, with the neat white blouse underneath. Smart, but not showy, like Angie herself. He wasn't sure about the higher than high-heeled court shoes or the garish gloss lipstick, but Angie spoke well and with conviction. She also seemed to have a good business head on her shoulders, a promising asset to a new multi-millionaire.

Smiling at this last thought, he lifted his head and caught Angie's eye. She gave him a searching look, but Dorothy shattered further thought.

Shifting in her wheelchair, her brisk tone intervened. "Let's move on. We have someone else to see soon."

Harold rose to see Angie out. Moving towards the front door, Angie wondered if she'd done enough to secure her place on the cruise. Dorothy's abrupt manner had unnerved her and gimlet stares and the irony of being on the end of the interrogation wasn't lost on her. Harold was another matter. She'd give it one last go.

Stepping over the doorstep, Angie turned and gave Harold a charming smile. "Thank you for seeing me today. I would *love* to be your cruise companion. Now I've met you, I know we'd both get more than just a book out of our time together."

She leaned in to kiss Harold on the cheek, then walked down the path, hips swinging. Transfixed, Harold stood in the doorway long after Angie had gone, gazing down the path, hand resting on the spot her lips had touched.

Dorothy's querulous voice reminded Harold the next candidate was due.

He sat opposite his mother, the still-warm seat reminding him of Angie. Flustered, he jumped up. "I liked her."

Taken aback by his tone, Dorothy looked up, her voice as firm. "Let's wait and see, shall we? There are four more on the shortlist and there's something about Miss Swan that I'm not sure about. I don't think she's quite what she seems."

"But *I* liked her," Harold insisted.

The front doorbell interrupted their exchange, signifying Debbie Jones's arrival.

After Angie's sparkle, Debbie appeared mousy, rather dowdy. Wearing smart suit and well-polished shoes, she'd clearly tried, but an unpleasant divorce and life as a single parent had taken its toll. The skirt and jacket were ill-fitting, as if she'd lost weight since buying. Despite discreet make-up, Dorothy detected signs of tiredness and stress. Dark circles under Debbie's eyes and thin lines at the side of her mouth.

Softening her voice, Dorothy told Debbie a bit more about life on board a luxury cruise ship.

As her interview drew to a close, Debbie asked, "What if it turned out we weren't getting on? Would we be stuck with each other throughout the cruise?"

Harold made to answer, but Dorothy was too quick for him. "No problem. You'd have to sort that out between yourselves. All you're committing to is lunch and dinner with Harold. You can go your own way the rest of the day if you want and we'll … he … will still pay for everything."

"It all sounds lovely. Being on my own and looking after the kids means I get little time to myself. A cruise would be heaven."

Harold gathered teacups and plates onto a tray and took them into the kitchen. Pressing his ear to the closed door, he made out muffled conversation.

Dorothy had lowered her voice. "Under no circumstances do you ask Harold how he's come into his money. Is that clear?"

Silence.

"And as far as the rest of the world's concerned, his identity remains secret. The only exception to that would be by prior agreement with him, although I can't imagine that happening. The successful applicant will sign a legally binding document and if she breaks the terms, we'll go straight to the courts. I'm sure you've had more than enough of lawyers."

Harold busied himself at the sink, then returned to the lounge to find Debbie standing up to leave.

"See Debbie out please, Harold. We've finished for now."

At the front door, Debbie whispered, "Your mum has it well organised, hasn't she?"

With a resigned look, Harold nodded, watching Debbie leave with none of the effects of Angie's departure. She was pleasant enough, but he felt she wanted more of a break from her children than a relationship with a man.

He returned to the lounge, speaking to Dorothy with an alien confidence. "That's that, Mum. Debbie was nice, but as far as I'm concerned, Angie would be great. I'd be happy to call the whole interviewing thing off and go with Angie."

Dorothy wouldn't hear of it. "Don't be daft, Harold. You must cast the net wider, see the rest of the shortlist."

"But I really don't want to." Harold's reluctance to the whole mad scheme returned.

As usual, Dorothy was a step ahead. "Tell you what, if that's how you feel, leave the rest of the applicants to me. I'll interview them. You needn't be there."

Harold protested. "I'm the one going on the cruise, the one having the companion."

"I know, I know." Dorothy adopted a sympathetic note, her look, understanding. "You've nothing to lose. Let me meet the others and I'll report back. You can meet the ladies if you like the sound of them."

Harold's heart sank, but he'd done enough rebelling for one day. "As you wish."

7

Tired as well as irritable, Harold woke with a start in the dark. Sticky with sweat, his heart raced, and a headache built behind his eyes. Raised on his elbow, he peered at the bedside clock: 3:37. Harold lay down again, mind in turmoil.

Escaping to a clifftop for reflection was all very well, but the way Harold felt, he wondered if jumping off would be better. So much had happened since that last walk. Since he'd declared Angie the winner after seeing only two applicants on the shortlist. Dorothy's upping of the pressure convinced Harold she'd taken leave of her senses. How else could he describe her crazy idea? In good humour, she'd suggested Harold take all five candidates. That way, if it didn't work out with one of them, he'd have others to choose from. Besides, apart from Angie, who'd clearly won him over with her charm and that special book offer, they were all deserving cases worthy of a break.

Debbie was getting over her nasty divorce, while savage cuts in the council's legal department had brought redundancy to newly qualified solicitor Annette. Recently widowed Chloe was anxious to get away following a road accident that robbed her of her husband, and Hannah's struggle to return to normality was understandable. Revenge porn courtesy of her ex-boyfriend resulted in a nervous breakdown.

Harold pondered at Dorothy's eagerness to load five women onto him. Doing that raised the possibility of losing the son she'd clung to for so long. She had always left him in no doubt that separation was the last thing she could consider. With such thoughts swirling around his head, Harold had no chance of getting back to sleep.

As dawn approached, darkness in the room had lightened to grey. Harold padded to the bathroom and squinted into the mirror. The face looking back wasn't a bad one, but were the pleasant, if nondescript features, worthy of attention from a woman? A wife even? He shrugged off his pyjamas and stepped into the shower, soaping himself before closing his eyes and tilting his head against the stream of steaming water.

From nowhere, a forgotten boyhood memory came to mind. Standing under the shower in the school gym after a game of rugby, buoyed by his success and his teammates' praise after scoring a try, he'd made a monumental decision. He was going to talk to the goddess.

He dried off, dressed, combed his fingers through damp hair and bared his teeth in the mirror to make sure nothing stuck between them. An afternoon of sport had given a healthy glow, and he recalled confidence surging. Grabbing his sports bag, he flung his satchel over his shoulder.

The boys' school playing fields were on the outskirts of Porthcoombe to the north. The girls' school lay to the west, and the roads from both converged by the bus station near the town centre. It was here, walking home from the games field, that he'd first spotted the goddess. Surrounded by a circle of girls in plaid skirt and blue blazer uniform, it was her blonde hair that caught his attention. Short and shining, sitting like spun gold on a slender, white neck. To his fevered adolescent brain, that hair turned her into the Aphrodite of his classical studies.

He'd spent the next few weeks desperate to time his walk home to coincide with her walk to the bus station so he could see her. He thought about the girl all the time and had a growing urge to get close to her, perhaps even speak to her. He lived for his next glimpse and when he missed her, despair overcame him.

His triumph on the rugby pitch coincided with a sighting, just as he'd hoped. To his delight, an omen maybe, the goddess was alone. He'd jogged across the road, satchel bumping against his back, and fell in beside her on the pavement. She didn't appear to notice him at first, but he didn't care. He couldn't think of a thing to say, instead imagining what it would be like telling the other boys about her or telling his parents he had a girlfriend.

At the bus station, she'd stopped and sneered at him. "Are you following me? What do you think you're doing? Get lost, loser."

With that, she swung herself onto the bus, turning on the top step to stick her tongue out and leaving him speechless. His goddess had feet of clay, shattering all hope.

A woman. Would he ever make the leap from fantasy to reality? How he'd react, handle the opportunity if it came his way, filled him with terror. That wasn't too strong a word. This was the chance of a lifetime versus the fear of the unknown. He'd probably make an utter fool of himself.

Today was Thursday, meaning a shift at the library before another day off tomorrow. *Damned cuts.* Dorothy had made it clear she was eager to move the cruise thing on. There was much to do. Harold had agreed to give his answer on the whole wretched thing by the weekend.

Opening his eyes, he stepped from the shower, and with renewed purpose, dried down. He'd head back to that clifftop early tomorrow morning, come home and give Dorothy his final decision.

8

This was not how it was supposed to be.

Harold's earlier resolve had crumbled. Today should be a full working day at the library, the perfect distraction for a while, banishing the all-consuming issue to the back of his mind. Instead, he operated on autopilot. Perfunctory smiles and pleasantries for colleagues and customers lacked their usual warmth and sincerity. People, especially those who knew him, gave puzzled stares. Not that Harold noticed, managing the enquiries desk while distracted.

First, Angie would not go away. Constant flashbacks of their last exchange on the doorstep. *Did she fancy him, or had he read too much into it?* Then Sandy competed for Harold's thoughts. Dorothy wouldn't tolerate the loss of her son to the woman on whom she depended. Besides, Sandy was far too attractive to be a potential girlfriend.

To his rescue came one of the library regulars. Even Harold, in his present state, couldn't fail to notice the overpowering combination of body odour and unwashed clothes. No one who came within sniffing distance of Cowboy Morris doubted he hadn't washed for weeks, maybe months. With an assortment of animals for company, he lived in a rickety old caravan, which a benefactor tolerated at the bottom of his sizeable garden. A stream ran nearby, which led anyone interested enough to speculate its suitability for some of Cowboy's essential life needs. Even if he got around to washing, chance was it would make little appreciable difference as he wore nothing other than ragged, grubby clothes, lurking under a filthy, old mac.

Every town, village, and public library had its collection of characters. People with few or none of life's conventional status symbols who fell into the category of lovable eccentrics. Cowboy Morris, maybe not lovable, was an eccentric, his well-spoken manner and apparent intellect in sharp contrast to his appearance.

"Would you be kind enough to give me the key to the old *Porthcoombe Gazettes,* please?" he requested.

Harold reached down to a drawer on the side of his desk and handed over the key. "Can I help you?" He knew what the answer would be, and the outcome. It was always the same whenever Cowboy used that library.

"No, thank you," Cowboy would say, only to return to Harold a few minutes later with a timid request. "I say, you couldn't give me a little help with this microfiche spool thing, please? My hands aren't at their best today, I'm afraid. I just can't get the film through the slots to set it all up."

When Harold set up the screen, Cowboy spent many hours combing through old copies of the *Gazette* for no obvious reason. Returning to his desk, Harold remained aware of Cowboy's presence. The old man kept up a continual low-level monologue, interspersed with hisses of breath taken in between clenched teeth and punctuated with exclamations of 'oh' and 'blimey, that clinches it.'

When disturbed, Cowboy lost all his charm, and it took all Harold's efforts to persuade him to let another user work the equipment. Cowboy's replacement sat down to do her own research. He strode around behind her, clutching his notepad, pen, and briefcase, his stink bludgeoning the nostrils of all those around him. Then he sat down next to the woman, huffed, puffed, and shuffled his papers.

Unable to contain himself any longer, Cowboy spoke. "Look, I'm sorry to bother you, Madam, but I'm engaged in the most frightfully important business with these old newspapers. Could you please allow me to resume my work?"

In silence, but with distaste clear on her face, the woman got up, glared at Harold, and stalked out of the library.

Years ago, Harold would have taken Cowboy to task for such behaviour, but he had long accepted the futility of this and couldn't be bothered today. He settled for sidling over. "Are you sure there's nothing more I can help you with?"

Cowboy said he was fine, thank you, but this time he couldn't resist speaking in hushed tones. "I am onto something, you know. I can't go public with it yet, but I'm damned if it's nothing short of a conspiracy. Yes, that's what it is, I tell you, a conspiracy."

Harold tried not to flinch as the old man grasped his arm, pulling him closer to his noisome figure. "Take it from me, young man. You must be wary. Things, including people, are often not what they seem."

9

Harold's clifftop escape was not as he'd envisaged—a beautiful sunrise over the sea with neither wind nor cloud. The reality was a stiff south-westerly wind driving rain into his face as his walking boots squelched along the muddied footpath. He had limited vision through rain-spattered lenses and there wasn't much to see anyway, low cloud and dense mist obscuring much of the coastline. At least his waterproofs kept all but his face dry and warm.

In similar past circumstances, he'd managed a little clear, constructive thinking. In fact, it was noticeable how one could switch off, no matter how bad the weather. You didn't have to be still to meditate; the key was to see nobody else. The moment you saw movement, distraction, and anticipated conversation, if only to say good morning, was the moment you were no longer with your thoughts. No chance of that this morning, with rain teeming and wind raging.

It mattered not, Harold reflected, arriving at his favourite spot and perching on a wet rock. He'd decided. No way was he going through with the whole madcap scheme. The fear factor had won. It was all too much. However luxurious, he would not be stuck on a cruise ship with five women for 18 days.

He wasn't sure about leaving Dorothy on her own, either. For all her domineering, irritating ways, he still loved her, and it would be the first time he'd parted from her for so long. His decision would no doubt disappoint his mother, given the vigour and passion she'd used in conceiving and organising the trip. Last night, she'd told him of her plans. The day before the cruise, she'd go off on a holiday of her own, spending three weeks with Linda, the spinster sister she hadn't seen in years. It was all doable, Dorothy insisted. There wasn't much they couldn't do for disabled people these days. She'd have VIP treatment and was looking forward to all the attention.

Mum can go ahead with that plan. I can look after myself for a while. Dorothy's breakout and reunion with her sister had been the something else she had to tell him. Harold didn't believe that. Something about the entire scheme and Dorothy's unprecedented passion that Harold may find himself a wife and leave her still didn't add up.

Cowboy Morris's words mattered not. Harold had made up his mind, and he didn't need to sit in this wretched weather and think any further. The cruise idea was dead.

10

Startled, Dorothy looked at Harold standing in the lounge doorway minus his boots, rain dripping from his waterproofs. "You're early."

"I'm wet, cold and need no more time to think. I've decided—"

"Yes, fine. Before you say anything else, take off those wet things and get a hot shower or you'll catch your death. When you're ready, you can make a pot of tea and join me."

After all the planning and effort she'd put in, Harold had expected stiff resistance, maybe outright hostility from his mother. She must have sensed his decision, although she seemed calm, indifferent even. After showering, Harold made tea, setting the tray on the coffee table. He noticed Dorothy's calm manner, as if at peace with everything, rather than on the brink of having all her plans dashed. A hint of a smile on her face, which far from putting Harold at ease, made him more nervous.

"I've reached my decision."

"Yes, of course you have, Harold, of course you have." Dorothy gestured to continue.

"I know you won't like this, but I've given it a great deal of thought and—"

"Oh, get on with it." Dorothy's smile stayed.

"I know you're looking forward to seeing Aunt Linda, but you can do that, anyway."

"We haven't got all day, you know."

"I've decided I'm not going on this cruise. I'm sorry, but I don't want to go. It's not me and I'm not going."

"Is that so?"

"Yes." Harold was as near to shouting at Mum as he'd ever been.

"That's a shame, isn't it, after we've told those five lovely young ladies they're going on a free cruise with you?"

"I am sorry."

Harold tried to steady his nerves by pouring tea, a tactic doomed to failure. His mother's cup and saucer clattered together, spilling tea onto the table. Dorothy remained impassive. No reaction to the spillage, nor the sight of her son's shaking hands.

Harold, trying to express a boldness he didn't feel, ventured, "If I wish to find myself a partner, I can take my time."

"Yes, yes, of course you can."

Why isn't she more annoyed, more animated?

"So, that's it, Mum. My last word."

Dorothy remained calm and fixed Harold with a long, amused look. "That's a bigger shame than you could imagine."

What is she up to?

"There's another young lady I've selected to join this cruise."

Harold's face dropped.

"She's delighted. Says she can't wait, thinks it's a wonderful idea."

Harold sensed a rise in temperature, sweat prickling his eyebrows and the back of his neck. He felt confused, worried, then a rapid unexpected sense of curious anticipation.

Dorothy swung around in her wheelchair. "I'll introduce the lady now. Sandy!"

11

The gleaming white *Gem of the Seas* dwarfed everything. At first sight, beyond the docks as the minibus tootled along, Harold experienced a rare surge of excitement.

Turning towards the Mayflower Cruise Terminal, he caught another glimpse of the towering ship. For a frightening moment, nausea wave zipped through his body. *She was colossal.* A floating tower block on many levels—capacity for 2,000 passengers, Dorothy said, and as many crew. Seven pairs of goggling eyes took in the scene, while the driver followed the steward's instructions, directing him to the drop-off point for Berth 106, Dock Gate 10.

The trip began four hours earlier, a minibus arriving to pick Harold up at 7am before collecting the others. When Dorothy told each female she wouldn't be Harold's sole companion, there was shock. However, no one changed their mind. Sitting upfront, Harold reflected on an ease among the six women. They introduced themselves and struck up excited chatter, everyone talking in unison throughout the journey. Harold contributed little to the conversation, speaking only when spoken to.

The bus halted, and conversation eased. Porters loaded and whisked away suitcases on trolleys, while Harold paid and tipped the driver. Hannah looked shocked as her luggage vanished.

Chloe tried to put her at ease. "Don't worry, everything's done for you. Next time you see that suitcase it'll be waiting outside your cabin."

Harold had used the long journey to consider the six women, whose happy prattle and assorted perfume worked his senses. Sandy was the one who'd tried to draw him into conversation. She had the sweetest nature and his spirits soared at the thought of spending time with her in the coming days.

On arrival at the terminal, Angie had given Harold another lingering look. She had something in mind, a strong hint of more than friendship, or that was how he read it. Consumed again by the women's conversation, Harold concluded that, save Sandy, his companions had forgotten the prime purpose of their trip. To accompany him.

Heading to a lounge before calling at check-in, the volume from the group rose again.

"We'll probably have to wait awhile because we're on Deck Nine. That's roughly in the middle of the passenger accommodation. The higher up you are, the sooner you're called," Chloe said.

"Goodness, you sound like an expert on these matters," Debbie said.

"A friend of mine's been on a few cruises. Apparently, check-in's quick, not like the hassle of an airport."

Chat subsided then out came mobile phones to report arrival at check-in. Harold noticed Angie was missing. He called Dorothy, who said she was enjoying her first full day away from home and asked after Aunt Linda. Dorothy said Linda was fine but couldn't speak to him as she'd gone shopping.

"Listen, Harold, there's no need to call every five minutes. I'm fine. For your sake, I want you to switch off from me for a while. Phone a couple more times before the cruise is over, nothing more."

A loudspeaker broadcast ticket numbers and colours and Harold's group headed to check-in for final formalities before that magic moment—boarding the majestic *Gem of the Seas.* Harold stood next to Hannah. She'd been giggling a lot but now clutched his arm when asked to look into a tiny camera.

"It's okay. I'm sure it's for security," Harold said.

Chloe confirmed. "That's right. The photograph's for your on-board cruise card used to pay for everything. It also acts as ID when you leave the ship and return."

Hannah tensed. "Oh, my God. Sorry, but I have a thing about cameras and photographs."

"Shame, as I'm sure there'll be lots of pictures taken over the coming days," Harold said, oblivious to the tortured expression on Hannah's face as he spoke.

The group didn't have long to wait. After progressing along a zigzag gangway tunnel, they boarded through a large, rectangular opening. A photographer greeted them.

"My, what have we here? Ladies, and gentleman, please, line up for your boarding shot. You'll see your photograph later in the ship's gallery, no obligation to buy, and—"

Before he could continue, Angie ushered the young man to one side. "Thanks, but no thanks. There's no need for your services. I'm a professional photographer and will record the cruise at every stage."

This was a departure from the script for the ship's snapper, who had no response. Angie swept the group forward, positioning them for her own photo.

She knows her business even if she's not in business yet. Harold mused at Angie's no-nonsense manner.

"Sorry. I haven't grasped everyone's names yet and need them for the caption. I must be sure of my facts. Names and spellings, please, left to right. Oh, and where you live. Town or village will do, and your age."

"Why do you need all that?" Annette asked.

"For the book I told you about on the way up, you know, the pictorial book of the cruise for Harold. I'll take as much detail as possible for now. I don't have to use it all if anyone's not happy."

Angie was about to put her camera, pen, and notebook into her bag when Annette returned to the fray.

"Pardon me, Angie, but if this is going to be a record of us on the cruise, what about you?"

Angie's defensive look was brief enough for Harold to miss, but not Annette. Agreeing, Angie forced a smile and assembled her tripod and camera. After setting the time delay, she rushed to join the group photo.

"What next?" asked Debbie, clapping her hands.

Chloe's excited voice rang out. "Let's see our cabins."

Debbie asked for directions and learned that cabins wouldn't be ready for another hour.

"Don't know about anyone else, but I'm bloody starving." What was fast becoming a trademark giggle accompanied Hannah's words.

Harold chipped in. "Yes, time for lunch. I reckon we should head to the buffet restaurant and tuck in."

Heads turned, seeking a uniformed helper to give directions, but no one was around.

Chloe to the rescue again. "Use the fold-up ship's map. It shows where everything is, what number deck and so on. There are bigger layout maps on the walls in the corridors."

Pocket maps opened and frantic movement erupted as 2,000 new passengers replaced the complement who'd disembarked hours earlier. In between, the minor miracle of a huge, rapid logistical operation ensuring the *Gem of the Seas* lay idle no longer than necessary. Tons of stores of all descriptions and several thousand suitcases stowed by crew hands. Housekeeping crews cleaning cabins and public areas, making up beds and distributing fresh towels, welcome hampers, and information leaflets. To keep the ship running, a large bunkering barge tied up alongside to refuel.

The group found the Roses Restaurant and sat down to eat in the open air on Deck 13 astern, high above one of the ship's four swimming pools. Harold muttered something about keeping room for the big dinner tonight, but his remark received short shrift from most companions. All but Annette and Sandy ended up with twice as much as they'd have for their main meal, including lashings of smoked salmon and prawns. They weren't alone. All around, fellow passengers tucked in.

Chloe forked up another mouthful of seafood. "Cruise passengers—according to my friend—eat for England and go home with a waist to show for it. They can't resist the fact you can eat all day. Determined to get their money's worth."

"We're going to stand out a mile." said Debbie.

Harold looked around, realising that as well as being older, many fellow cruisers shared the jowled appearance of good-living untouched by temperate habits and gym sessions. Food and drink were plentiful, attentive waiters quick to spot an empty glass. Hannah immediately ordered a beer. The others looked at Harold, who reassured.

"Go ahead, please. They're all on me—right through the cruise, remember."

Relaxing and enjoying their drinks, Angie said nothing but regarded Harold over the top of her glass. Feeling her eyes on him, he shifted in his seat.

Breaking the awkwardness, Hannah pushed back her seat. "Let's find our cabins. Think they'll be ready now, don't you?"

"How do we get to them from here?" asked Debbie.

"Maps. Don't worry, soon we'll be intimate with it all," said Chloe.

This remark, especially *intimate*, played on Harold's mind as he entered his cabin. He dropped his case and took in the accommodation. Bright from a glittering central chandelier and assorted table lamps to his left, a sumptuous bathroom with walk-in shower, jet tub, and piles of thick white towels. To the right, a small sofa and chair and a table holding a vase of pink lilies scenting the cabin. Sliding doors, gently billowing dark blue curtains framing balconied seating.

The major feature was the bed, the biggest Harold had ever seen. Made up with spotless white linen and dressed in piles of plump pillows, a silk runner of dark blue, and matching bolsters, it dominated the room. Opulent, inviting, shouting indulgence and intimacy.

Harold closed his eyes, visions of sharing such a bed floating in his head.

12

Late afternoon and the cruise was underway. Fascinated, Harold watched crew slip the moorings fore and aft from the dockside, winching them aboard. Detaching from the dockside, the great ship floated away.

There was no real sense of motion, no change of sound. Ashore, a handful of dock workers, did nothing in particular. One movement Harold couldn't miss in his peripheral vision was a mass of radiant auburn hair. Chloe sidled up.

"I'm told they used to make a much bigger thing of this. A band playing on the quayside, colourful streamers flying down, free champagne."

"It's probably the cuts. There is a Grand Sailaway party—saw an invitation in my cabin. Maybe they'll serve champagne there."

"I expect drinks won't be free. Why don't we find out? According to the invite, the party's a couple of decks down at the stern."

Uncomfortable, Harold shuffled. "No thanks. I'm not a party person. I'd rather watch from up here where it's quiet."

"Oh, come on, at least try it. I suspect the other girls will be there, too. It won't be a proper party. Everything'll be out in the open. A great send-off to get everyone in the mood."

Before Harold could reply, Chloe hooked her arm in his.

"All right. Just for a few minutes."

A muffled thrum of loud music told them they were on the right deck. Harold opened the door for Chloe, deafening noise hitting the couple. Crowds of cruisers waving plastic Union Jacks danced around the swimming pool and members of the ship's entertainment team, dressed in white and dotted among the dancers, encouraged the party atmosphere. The DJ spotted Harold and Chloe and maintained his hearty line of communication.

"Here we have another couple for a piece of the action. Come on. Let's see you hit the dance floor."

Once again, Chloe tugged at Harold's arm, but this time his resistance was stronger and he held firm, saying nothing but shaking his head. Chloe sensed his discomfort and had the good sense not to push. Instead, the couple sat on the side of an empty sun lounger. A server asked if they'd like a drink.

Chloe ordered a pina colada. Harold declined.

Shouting to make himself heard, he explained his decision. "I'm not a great drinker. Not teetotal, but not silly. I'll look forward to having wine with dinner tonight."

Chloe shrugged. A young man in white thrust Union Jacks at the couple.

"Come on, Harold, we're supposed to wave these. You can do that at least."

Harold turned to reply, shaken by the look on Chloe's face. Once happy, it now crumbled. To his horror, she was on the verge of tears. He stayed quiet until the moment passed.

Chloe gulped. "Sorry."

Wrapped in white robes and towelled heads, Angie and Hannah's arrival saved Harold from having to speak.

Angie teased. "Hey, party-poopers, what are you doing sitting here? It got so hot on the dance floor, we had to throw ourselves in the pool. Seems you're not entering the spirit of things yet."

Hannah chipped in. "You're supposed to wave the flags. Come on, wave, and think of England. Like this." Giggling, she took Harold's wrist.

The girls sat down, eyeing Chloe's drink.

Hannah couldn't stop herself. "Oh, my God, that looks bloody lovely. Can I have a sip?"

Without waiting for a reply, she snatched the glass and sucked on the straw. "Yes, please," she said to the server, who nodded and turned to Angie.

"And you, Madam?"

"The same."

Hannah jumped up, pulled the towel from her head, and dropped her robe on the floor revealing bright pink hair, a lime-green halter-top bikini and silver belly-button ring. She danced over to Chloe. Come on. Let's boogie. Dance with me."

Laughing, Chloe joined her. Harold watched them bopping around the deck, struck by their lack of inhibition, fascinated by a tattoo on Hannah's neck. He turned to Angie, who was reading the cocktail menu.

"This isn't my scene. I'll leave you to it."

"I'll come with you."

Harold resisted. "You stay here, sip your cocktail and enjoy the dancing. I'll see you all at dinner tonight."

Angie kissed him on the cheek before he could escape. "Okay. See you later."

Harold almost ran to Deck 13, away from the noise, the music, the girls. Finding an open area stretching from port to starboard, he had a grandstand view of the sail down the Solent. There were a couple of other people in the vicinity but no one close enough to talk to, so he focused on the Isle of Wight, recovering his breath and wits. Reliving the kiss, a warm glow consumed him. Catching Angie's hot breath, the sweet sensation of warm, soft lips brushing his skin. With sea taking over from land and the sharp tang of salty air in his lungs, Harold cooled from the memory and got to thinking. His old fears returned. *He was hours away from dinner with six female companions.*

He returned to his cabin to relax. Tonight's dress code was casual. He liked the idea of dressing up for dinner on board ship. Pity that was on its way out, along with a host of other traditions. Dress code was the least of his worries. His mother aside, he'd never dined with one woman, let alone six. One thing was certain. Anxiety and a loss of appetite wouldn't affect his waistline during this cruise.

13

Sensing eyes on him, Harold led his six companions to table 92 to be greeted and seated.

In reality, most diners were talking to each other or consumed in reading the extensive menu, salivating at the culinary delights. A few curious people turned their heads, especially when the ladies' exchanges powered into overdrive. Seated between Angie and Sandy, Harold couldn't help looking at an elderly man sitting nearby, with a woman Harold assumed was his wife. The man had hobbled into the restaurant on crutches, supporting what appeared to be prosthetic legs.

"You okay there, Tyler?" the woman asked.

"Course I am," the man snapped in an American accent, scowl intensifying as attentive servers watched his every move.

Harold focused on his table, where everyone busied themselves ordering. To start, Harold opted for chicken liver parfait, a dish he'd never tasted before. It sounded indulgent; his steak main conjuring up the same image. The sommelier introduced himself as being at their service for the duration of the cruise, recommending the group take advantage of the wine package offer, committing to a set number of bottles for the trip.

"Yes, please," Hannah enthused.

Mischievous, Angie turned to Harold. "I'm sure that won't be an issue for a man of your means."

Harold forced a smile.

Annette, who'd drawn up the terms of the cruise companion arrangement, chipped in. "I thought we'd all agreed to make no reference to that."

"Sorry." Angie's tone was insincere.

Harold ordered three bottles of wine. Giggling, Hannah suggested they should have taken six.

"No. I won't be drinking much," Harold insisted.

The sommelier nodded, moved away, and the volume of happy, excited voices resumed. In silence, Harold studied his guests.

Angie and Hannah had most to say. At random, Angie gripped Harold's wrist and tried to draw him into the conversation without success. Much to Harold's alarm, the loudest, Hannah, was already tipsy. Debbie's contributions, fewer but to the point, had an edge, while Sandy joined the laughter rather than initiating conversation. Despite this, Harold felt a comforting presence at his side.

Authoritarian, Annette fixed Chloe with a stare straight out of a courtroom. "Come on, give more insights into cruising. Something else your friend has told you."

Harold tensed as the others turned to Chloe. For a moment, she looked uneasy. Service of the first course and a chorus of gleeful approval intervened.

Feeling bold, Harold spoke. "Bon appétit, ladies. I have an idea in mind for you all."

Harold speaking, let alone talk of an idea, was enough to make everyone fall silent and listen.

Feeling more relaxed and confident, Harold spoke again. "I'll tell you when we've finished our starters, while waiting for the next course."

"Ooh, you tease," said Angie, taking another opportunity to snuggle up and rub her cheek against the top of his arm.

Harold pulled away.

"Tell us now."

Harold was aware of several heads turning their way at Hannah's brash tone and giggle. Too loud for his liking.

He retorted with a look of mock concern. "Ladies, ladies, please behave or I won't tell you at all."

After starters, Harold drew breath. "Now for my idea if you'd all like to take part. As we're new to each other and will be together for meals over the next few days, I'd like you to give a brief introduction. Whatever you'd like to say—work, personal or both, but you must say as much as you can about yourself in less than five minutes."

"Oh, gawd, has Annette drawn up a contract for that as well?" asked a glassy-eyed Hannah.

Annette and Harold ignored the interruption, Harold inviting Angie to start. She did, with confident ease, repeating the story she'd told Dorothy about her aspirations to set up a photography business and the pictorial book she had in mind for the cruise.

Hannah and Sandy applauded; Chloe smiled. Harold noticed Annette and Debbie's puzzled expressions.

After the soup course, Harold looked at Debbie. "Are you ready?"

Debbie made to stand.

"No, no, please stay in your seat. Nothing formal."

"Sorry. Habit of mine after my previous job as a project manager with a property development company. Yes, women can do everything these days."

Her audience cheered, again attracting looks from other diners.

"Thank you, thank you. Sometimes, I would double up as marketing manager, which involved formal address. I also gave acceptance speeches when collecting awards on behalf of the company."

"Well done, you."

As far as Harold could make out, Hannah's interruption was sincere.

"Ah, but the company was struggling and cutting back, that's why I did so much."

"Right. Come on, let's hear about your personal life," Hannah said.

Debbie gave a tolerant smile. "I have two lovely children—Lisa, who's seven, and four-year-old Jason. I took maternity leave, but my husband and I split, got divorced then I gave up my job. The company was failing and frankly, it was a bloody awful time. At one stage, I became suicidal."

"Know the feeling," said Hannah.

"Think I'm finally coming out the other side. That's why I applied for this opportunity. A clean break, let this cruise launch my new life. Sounds grand, I know, but that's how I feel."

Warm smiles all around and a burst of applause. Angie reached over and hugged Debbie.

Harold smiled. "Thanks, Debbie. Annette?"

Annette took a sip of wine. "I'm a solicitor. I read law at Cardiff University and started my first job working in the county council's legal department. Months later, there were cuts across the board and a round of redundancies. No department was safe. Last in, first out. I had to go. I finished a few weeks ago and don't know what I'm going to do now. These days, vacancies are scarce. I've thought about setting up on my own but don't have the capital."

For a moment, sharp-eyed Harold saw Annette's eyes settle on him when delivering the last comment.

"Away from work, when I was in work, that is—"

"Yeah, we've got the message, Annette darling," Hannah cut in.

"You'll all have to forgive me if I sound bitter about life right now. Away from work, I'm a keen swimmer and took part in competitive diving with some success. I'm also into freediving—going underwater for as long as I can while holding my breath. I've managed a depth of forty-five metres and back using my weight and a monofin."

This revelation silenced Hannah before mumbling, "Crumbs. I never learned to swim."

"I'm also a quiz addict. You'll find me at every quiz on this cruise." With a smile and a modest shrug of the shoulders, Annette concluded. "That's all, folks."

"Thank you, Annette. Ah, the mains," Harold said.

Angie took several photos as the delighted group enthused over plates of beautifully presented food. Harold's steak was the indulgence he'd pictured. Rich, succulent, with mouth-watering Bearnaise sauce, fresh vegetables, and golden fries just how he liked them— crisp on the outside, soft to the bite.

"Okay, Chloe. What can you tell us about yourself?"

"And don't forget to give us more cruise insights from your *friend*," Annette suggested.

"I set up business as a florist, working from home. I've always loved flowers, so thought I'd give it a go. Wedding bouquets, funeral wreaths, birthdays, Valentine's and so on. It's a competitive market. The business hasn't done well of late."

Faces dropped, and Harold feared an outburst from a fidgeting, bored-looking Hannah.

"I've also suffered bereavement after my husband died in a car crash. Things have been difficult, and I'm hoping this cruise will pick me up again. Get me away from everything."

Fighting back tears, Chloe's voice tailed off and there was silence around the table. Seeing formidable Annette taking Chloe's hand surprised Harold. Even Hannah said nothing.

"Coffee?" A waiter relieved the atmosphere.

"Hannah. Your turn now, please," Harold said.

"I studied at Falmouth School of Art. It took ages to get a job. Eventually, a graphic design company took me on and I dealt with many jobs, including branding, posters, and web graphics."

She stopped talking. Harold noticed her leg bouncing up and down, hands in tight fists on the table.

Hannah's voice became louder, bitter. "It all went wrong after my disastrous relationship. Mentally, I got myself into a weird place and lost my job. It didn't make the papers, thank Christ, but I posed nude for the ex, who took photos. Then we broke up."

Heads around the room turned in disapproval and annoyance. Among them, the American's, but Harold registered mild amusement and sympathy in his gaze. The ship's staff looked concerned.

"Hannah, please," Harold said.

Hannah ignored him. "You might as well all know. Half the bloody world already does since he posted the photos on the internet. He was a crap guy. We had a crap relationship. Life's been shit since. Nervous breakdown, secure unit, the lot."

Oblivious to looks from the other diners and the shocked silence of her companions, a sobbing Hannah slumped back in her chair.

"Can I interest you in any liqueurs, ladies, and gentleman?" enquired the sommelier, as if nothing was amiss.

"Brandy," said Hannah.

Harold looked at his watch. "We've run out of time and should move if we want to make the theatre for the show."

Hannah frowned, but Chloe reassured her. "Don't worry, lovey, there'll be staff in the theatre ready to serve drinks. Get your brandy there."

Annette's disapproval showed.

As the party stood to leave, Harold whispered to Sandy. "Sorry we didn't have time for your introduction tonight."

He couldn't help noticing her relief and said no more, making a mental note to try again tomorrow.

14

Thanking Harold, both Annette and Debbie were ready for bed after a long, busy day. Sandy said she'd give the show a miss, offering Harold a warm smile, enough to convince him she was contemplating a kiss before thinking better of it. Before she moved away, Harold kissed her on the cheek.

"Thanks for a lovely day, Harold." Sandy's face sparkled.

For a precious moment, Harold felt on top of the world, a reaction not lost on Angie. The rest of the group headed to the theatre for the show. Hannah had her brandy; Angie ordered a beer. Chloe and Harold declined more drink. Despite enjoying the show, Harold nodded off near the end. Angie gave up prodding him and didn't resist when his head rested against her shoulder. At the end of the show, he felt embarrassed when she gave him a gentle shake.

"Come on, Harold. Show's over, time to go."

"We're not going to bed yet, are we? The night's still young, let's go to the disco," Hannah said.

Harold and Chloe made it clear they were not up for disco dancing.

Imploring, Hannah tugged at Angie's arm. "Come on, the night's young. Come with me, please."

"Okay."

The theatre emptied, with Harold right behind Hannah. As they went their separate ways, Hannah's lovely smile had such warmth that Harold forgot all the discomfort she'd caused in the restaurant. When she ran to kiss his cheek and thank him, he felt a surge of affection for her.

A second kiss, this time from Angie, felt less impetuous and more practised, especially when accompanied by an artful look. "Thanks so much for a great day, Harold. See you tomorrow."

Harold went to his cabin, Chloe beside him. All seven cabins were adjoining on Deck 9, Chloe's, two down from his.

In the corridor outside Harold's cabin, Chloe kissed his cheek.

"I'm sorry about tonight. You know … when I broke down."

"Don't worry, forget about it."

Chloe looked up and down the corridor. "Thank you, but there's something I haven't told you about myself. Maybe I'll tell you before the cruise is over. I hope I can." She thanked him again and headed off.

A single, soft light glowed in Harold's cabin, the bed turned down, a goodnight chocolate placed on a pillow. Chloe's closing remarks had puzzled him. Munching the sweet treat, Harold's thoughts turned to Cowboy Morris's warning, an unsettling reminder that didn't stay long. He was asleep in seconds.

15

Harold's breathing was intense. Angie, and Hannah either side of him, Chloe stroking his head, Debbie and Annette looking on from the foot of the bed.

Sandy appeared at the door. She didn't look happy. "You know I have always loved you, Harold."

Soon, she stood beside him at his favourite spot—on the cliffs, looking down at the churning sea. Harold turned to kiss her. As their lips met, Sandy tumbled off the cliff.

Panting, Harold woke up and looked at his bedside clock. Just after six. With breakfast a while off, he showered and decided on the perfect start to the new day. He'd enjoy the sea air on the top deck and walk a few circuits of the ship. He'd worked out that 3.3 circuits equalled one mile.

The *Gem of the Seas* was silent save for the ever-present hum of engines. Harold saw no one as he climbed four flights of stairs, disappointed to be short of breath. He pinched his waistline. With three weeks of high living ahead, he promised himself he wouldn't gain more weight. Walking would help burn calories. *Could there be a more exhilarating start to the day?* Harold mulled the question as a stiff sea breeze hit his cheeks and he admired the breathtaking spectacle of the vast sea. Even at this early hour, it surprised him other walkers and runners had beaten him to it.

He started at the briskest pace he could muster, much better for his heart than strolling. Yes, he'd do this every morning, he vowed, striding past a netted golf practice range, tennis court, a couple of swimming pools and the ship's enormous funnel. Apart from one cruiser, everyone he saw said a hearty good morning. He heard footsteps catching up with him, then familiar clipped tones.

"Hello, Harold, fancy seeing you here."

"Sandy." He turned around.

She continued to run on the spot, Harold taken by the vision of glowing health and athleticism, so different from her usual aspect as his mother's carer.

"What are you?" He laughed, changing tack: "I guess it's obvious what you're doing here at this time of morning."

Sandy smiled, saying nothing.

"I didn't know you were into running."

"I was not. I started after finding out about the cruise. Don't want to gain weight with good food and wine. Your mum paid for my gear."

"I see. About that introduction last night, I'm sorry we ran out of time. We must do it at dinner tonight."

A frown replaced the smile. "Actually, Harold."

"Yes?"

"I would rather we did not. Please."

Sandy wore a troubled expression, making Harold sympathetic, puzzled. "All right, no problem."

He conceded, with reluctance, wanting to probe, but decided now was not the time. Instead, he delighted in returning Sandy's warm smile.

"Don't let me keep you. Off around the ship or you might seize up."

"I go," she said.

Harold looked after the running figure, still astonished at Sandy's changed appearance. As she disappeared around the ship's forward superstructure, Harold's overwhelming thought remained. *I just want to scoop her up and wrap her in love.*

In no time, Sandy was back alongside him, asking what his plans were for that day.

"I might ring Mother."

"No need for that. She wants to give you a break, leave you in peace for a while."

Sandy was hasty in her plea, it seemed.

"Maybe I'll drop her an email. I'll have a session on the internet in the ship's cyber suite."

A self-confessed Luddite, Harold despised the move to automated, impersonal systems in his library. He refused to activate the email and internet options on his phone. Immobile and removed from the outside world, Dorothy was the opposite.

Sandy smiled. "I'm on my last lap. I look forward to seeing you at lunchtime if not before."

After breakfast in a quiet buffet restaurant, Harold bought himself an hour's time on the web. Only a day since he'd started his holiday, but he wished to keep abreast of news back home. Finding nothing of interest on the *Porthcoombe Gazette's* website, he browsed *Cornwall Clarion*, shocked by two pieces of news.

More library cuts across county

As part of a fresh round of major public spending cuts, Cornwall Council announced a reduced programme of services in its libraries, with further cutbacks to opening hours and redundancy warnings. Reduced hours will start next Monday, and the cash-strapped authority is reviewing all aspects of its library services.

'It's with extreme regret we can't rule out a small number of redundancies,' a council spokesperson said.

Dumbfounded, Harold read about self-service kiosks, increased online resources and the possibility a commercial organisation may take over handling the service. Slumped in his chair, he failed to take in the news, couldn't believe the radical changes and quick implementation. He wanted to cry.

As a distraction, he scrolled through the pages, another headline staggering him.

16

Horrified, Harold located the report and gaped at the screen. Though brief, the content made him sweat.

Massive lottery jackpot winner?

Following the announcement of one of the biggest ever EuroMillions wins—more than £120m—rumours persist that the jackpot winner is a man from the Porthcoombe area of Cornwall. The winner chose no-publicity, but local speculation has intensified in recent weeks, following an advertisement in the personal column of a Cornish newspaper for a cruise companion.

For an 18-day cruise to Venice, the advertiser was, 'seeking a female companion for the duration—and maybe longer.' Inviting applications from interested women, he promised, 'to cover the total cost of the cruise and all related expenses.'

Do you know the lottery winner? Do you know the lucky lady chosen for the holiday of a lifetime?

We'd love to hear from you. Meanwhile, speculation continues!

Dazed, Harold could only stare. *Has one of his companions leaked the story? Who hasn't revealed her true identity?*

A flash on the screen told Harold ten minutes' computer time remained. He bought another hour, accessing his email account to message his mother, including links to the two news reports:

Hi, Mum.

What do you make of these?

Love,

Harold x

Within minutes, Dorothy replied:

Let's talk about library cuts later.

Regarding the lottery report, I'm as shocked as you are, but it's speculation and the only thing resembling substance is the reference to our advert.

As for a spy among the six women, I think that's a little far-fetched, although I had my suspicions about one of them. That's me being paranoid.

In all senses, Harold, switch off.

Love,

Mum x

Despite Dorothy's assurances, Harold's panic at the *Clarion's* website revelation remained. He wondered which of the six his mother suspected. He had time left on the computer but closed it down, leaving the credit for another session. On the deck, Harold browsed four pages of the ship's daily events and settled on his morning schedule. First, more walking, then coffee at an outside table overlooking the swimming pool and the ship's wake stretching back towards the horizon. After, the port lecture, previewing the first stop ashore at Cadiz.

At lunch, he'd take a renewed interest in every word, deed, and scrap of body language from his six companions.

17

E mail from Roy Carter to Angie Swan:

Hi, Angie,

How's it going? Anything of interest to report?

I'm sending a link to show you what the opposition's come up with. If the *Clarion* sticks with it and/or others follow, we'll need to work fast to get a story, and by that, I mean *the* story. Start working on Harold as soon as you can and keep me informed of developments.

Regards.

Roy

Reply from Angie:

Thanks, Roy. Wow. No idea where that came from.

I've held off from Harold so far. I think he's sweet on one of the women (his mum's carer). He's got his work cut out with one of the bunch, bit of a headcase, who,

I suspect, may cause trouble before long. My instincts tell me Harold fancies me, too.

Keep you posted. Best wishes.

Angie

18

At a crowded buffet restaurant, Harold arrived for lunch, unsure whether he'd locate his companions. Darting here and there, people piled food high on plates. One would think they hadn't eaten for days. Constant replenishment of every item on the menu meant there was plenty to go around, plenty of time to enjoy. Seating for everyone, too, especially with the overspill in the open-air section, a definite option in today's sunshine.

Above the din, Harold heard familiar voices. He turned his head, not immediately concerned at Hannah's absence. Collecting a tray, he headed to the food counters to load his lunch and returned to the table to eat. Greeted by the smiling five, Harold clocked Angie seated opposite, giving him a prolonged gaze.

"How's it going, ladies?"

A chorus of enthusiastic responses.

"This lunch part of the itinerary is pretty informal, isn't it? Maybe we should abandon the idea of meeting up for lunch and do our own thing during the day. If some meet up anyway, that's fine, but I think it's fairer and better if we all have freedom in the daytime. Don't forget, you can book whatever shore trips you want on my account. The only definite will be our eight-thirty dinner in the Ruby Restaurant. What do you think?"

Agreed, with a mix of politeness and enthusiasm.

"I reckon the contracts could survive that variation of terms." Annette spoke with mock gravity.

Angie wasn't keen on the idea. "If you don't mind, Harold, I'd be happy to meet up with you for lunch and dinner. That way, we can keep tabs on progress with the photographs and your book."

"Fine by me. I'm usually here around twelve-thirty if all else is equal. On that subject, I may as well tell you what my default routine will be while at sea, in case any of you need to know. Of course, you're always welcome to join me anytime."

"Yes, sir." Chloe saluted.

"Even dinner comes with a little caveat, another idea involving a slight variation to the arrangement. I'll tell you tonight and think—hope—you'll like it."

Harold was pleased to see the stir his comments caused, feeling amused by whispered exchanges as the women tried to guess what he wanted to tell. He didn't want to spoil the atmosphere but had to ask something and cleared his throat.

"I see there's a no-show from Hannah. Anyone know where she is, or how she is? Anyone seen her this morning?"

Angie hesitated, then said. "She had a lot to drink last night at dinner, and a few more at the disco. I left her there about half-twelve."

Harold looked at Angie in a way that said he knew her story was incomplete.

"I left her absorbed with one of the entertainment team."

"Okay. Thanks, Angie. I'll see if I can find her after lunch."

After trying Hannah's mobile and giving up his search of the ship, Harold tried her cabin. There was no reply when he knocked on the door. He went to his cabin and called her cabin number, about to hang up, when a groggy voice grunted.

"Hannah, is that you?"

"Yeah."

"It's Harold. We missed you at lunch. Are you okay?"

"Lunch?"

"Yes, lunch."

A long pause.

"Are you still there?"

"What time is it?"

"Two in the afternoon."

"Oh, hell."

"It's okay. As long as you're all right."

"Sorry, Harold, made a bit of a night of it. Had no idea it was so late."

"In that case, if I don't see you before, I'll look forward to seeing you at dinner tonight."

Another long pause followed by a deep sigh and a growled, "Yeah, okay."

The receiver went down with a crash.

Hannah didn't turn up for dinner. Concerned or relieved? After the previous night's experience, Harold didn't know which to be. A text message told him she didn't feel up to the formal meal and was having a bite in the buffet restaurant instead. No one commented on her absence and judging by the volume of laughter and conversation around the table, she wasn't missed. Harold looked at animated faces and felt his resolve falter. Was one of these bright, happy women an informer? Only one way to find out.

"Ladies."

No one heard him, so Harold tried again.

Again no response.

Harold sat up in his seat, saying with surprising authority, "Could I have your attention, ladies, please?"

This had the desired effect, and five attentive faces looked his way. Harold blushed, squirmed in his seat, and plunged in.

"Does the *Cornwall Clarion* newspaper mean anything to any of you?"

Harold noted only Angie reacted. The others looked puzzled. For a second, he thought he detected a defensive expression on Angie's face, as if she'd been caught off guard, but recovered her poise.

Hesitantly, Harold continued. "Okay, so no one's been in touch with that newspaper lately?"

Again, puzzled frowns, shaking heads.

"Nobody's tipped them off about anything?"

The same response, and this time a question from Annette. "What are you driving at, Harold?"

Aware of their scrutiny, and rattled by Annette's directness, Harold faltered. "Well, you see ..."

Puzzled faces fixed on him.

"It's nothing. I don't want to talk about it if no one knows what I'm talking about."

"This is cryptic, Harold," said Chloe.

"Yes, I know. Apologies."

Harold turned to Angie. "You don't work for the *Clarion,* do you?"

A bland expression replaced a flash of confusion on Angie's face. Leaning back in her chair, she crossed her arms. "No, of course not. Whatever gave you that idea?"

"The photographs you've taken and personal details you've had from us."

"You know why I'm doing that. For your book." Angie hoped her voice was calm.

"Yes, of course. Sorry."

Feeling his temperature rising, Harold hadn't reckoned on what would follow next.

Sensing her first opportunity, Angie turned defence into attack. "Your questions aren't anything to do with a big lottery winner by any chance, are they?"

Feeling the situation escaping his control, Harold couldn't summon a reply.

"You're out of order there, Angie." Annette's stern tone was enough.

"Sorry."

Nervous, Harold bought time, reaching for his glass while around the table others fiddled and twitched. Relief came from an unexpected quarter.

"Everyone, *please*. Let's give our wonderful host a chance. We have a free cruise and in return we agreed no questions, remember?" Sandy smiled.

"Agreed," said Angie.

Harold couldn't make out whether Angie was withdrawing or building up to another attack.

She paused, then resumed. "Confession time. I wasn't entirely truthful. I saw the *Clarion* report on the internet, but my first instinct was to say nothing about it for fear of embarrassing Harold."

Setting off another round of chatter, Angie's words washed over Harold as he recovered poise.

"Can we move on to the second subject I want to talk about?" he said.

There was a palpable sense of relief around the table.

"I'd like to get to know you better and invite each of you to dine with me at the Azure."

Advertised as a superior, exclusive restaurant with only 20 tables, The Azure required advance booking. Glowing faces gave Harold confidence to continue.

"I'll take that as a yes. Now, it's a question of who's first. Any suggestions?"

Annette, Chloe, and Debbie all made to raise their hands, but Angie was quicker.

"I'm game, Harold, so I can say a *special* sorry for that little lapse of mine just now." Angie softened her voice, the emphasis not lost on Harold.

"Thank you, but I'll make you second if you don't mind."

Angie's face dropped, but Harold continued, looking serious once more.

"I'd like to take Hannah first, if I can find her. I want to find out what her problem is, see if I can help her. That's best done in the privacy of a quiet restaurant. Hope you understand. I want to draw her out when she doesn't have an audience to play to. Enjoy yourselves while I'm in the Azure tomorrow night and keep your fingers crossed. I suspect the experience will be more than interesting."

19

Email from Angie Swan to Roy Carter:

Hi, Roy,

I'm sure Harold is the lottery winner. Can't substantiate anything yet, but it's a start. I'm having a private dinner with him soon, which I hope will reveal more.

Best wishes.

Angie

Reply from Roy Carter:

Thanks, Angie,

You'll have to gain his confidence to get anything to stack up. That's before we reach the decision on whether to run a story. Remember, he's gone to great lengths to preserve his anonymity, and you've signed a legal document to say you'll never reveal his identity unless permitted.

Odds still against you, but well done for now. Be careful, be clever and keep me informed.

Regards.

Roy

20

Hannah gawked at the room. "Wow! This is a bit posh."

In the Azure, the maître d' bowed to her and pulled out a chair at the table covered in a pristine white cloth. Gesturing her to sit, he lit the pink candle accompanying a single red rose and introduced the table and wine waiters. With a flourish, he handed elaborate menus to both Hannah and Harold.

Giddy with the attention and the unexpected glamour of her surroundings, Hannah giggled. "It's almost as big as me."

She propped the menu on the table and mouthed the unfamiliar words, running a red fingernail along the lines of print. Harold studied her.

In a scarlet red floor length dress, shiny, thin material highlighted Hannah's generous figure, a side split revealing solid legs in silver platform-heeled sandals. The dress's plunging neckline afforded a show of ample bosom. Harold decided Hannah had tried for a classy look that ended up reflecting her loud, attention-grabbing character, both of which concerned him. He caught her eye over the top of her menu.

"What are you thinking, Harold? Dad looks at me like that sometimes. Like I'm a hopeless case, you know?" She laughed, then hiccupped.

"What does your father do?"

"He's a businessman. Has a lot of companies, swish car. Divorced from Mum when I was a kid. Don't hear from her much. She has a drink problem, but Dad looks after me well enough."

"In what way?"

"Always there when I need him. Bails me out when required. He's done that a few times. He'd do anything for me, even fly out for me, or arrange my transfer back home if I get fed up with this cruise."

"I hope that won't be necessary."

"Hey, Harold, we can have a different wine with every course."

He was aghast. They'd both had a couple of pre-dinner cocktails in the bar. Hannah had also enjoyed several beers with her lunch.

"I'm not sure after those cocktails," he said.

Hannah wore a lopsided grin. "Rubbish. Live a little. I fancy the cheese soufflé starter. I'll have red with that, then white with lobster and a lovely dessert wine to finish."

"I'm not a big drinker."

"You wouldn't leave me drinking all on my own, would you? Keep me company, Harold."

"If that's what you want."

"Do you know something?" Hannah was in a playful mood.

"What?"

"We never got to hear your introduction."

"No, and you're not going to, although I'm happy to divulge a little to each of you one-to-one. Anyway, I want to find out more about you. That's why I chose you first."

Glassy-eyed, Hannah regarded Harold with pursed lips. She leaned across the table. "You want to know how I came to be starkers on the internet, don't you? How I became a revenge porn victim?"

Harold raised his hands, but Hannah ploughed on, looking around the restaurant before speaking in a loud voice.

"Don't suppose this ship, with all its services, stretches to a shrink, does it?"

Harold winced, aware of heads twisting their way.

"No, Hannah, it doesn't."

"That's where I was for a while before this cruise. In shrinkville, I mean. Think your mum must've taken pity on me. Don't know why else I'd be here. It was her doing, wasn't it?"

Harold nodded.

"This cruise is supposed to be the start of my big comeback. I'm sure you recall me telling you at dinner the other night, everything went wrong for me. My life turned to shit."

Harold flinched. There was no stopping Hannah.

"After jerk man posted those nude pictures on the internet, it was a nervous breakdown for me. Psychiatric treatment, loss of job, the lot."

She was diverted by the waiter arriving with starters and tucked into her cheese soufflé. "This is yummy."

Harold toyed with his seafood cocktail, wondering what further revelations lay ahead. He figured he may as well get it over with as soon as possible. "You seem keen to talk about it. Why did you pose for the photos and why did your boyfriend post them on the internet?"

Hannah threw a contemptuous look. "It made me feel desirable. Respected."

"Respected?"

Frowning, Hannah twiddled her spoon around the remnants of soufflé. "There's nothing more important than your body, especially for a woman. I don't have a model figure, so it felt good to know that this guy wanted to photograph my body."

"But you've referred to him as jerk man more than once. Why weren't you more cautious?"

"Because that was before things went off. Before I found out what a jerk he was. I didn't see it coming. I did first and thought later. Should have been the other way around." Hysteria crept into Hannah's voice.

"You must have realised that once the photos existed, there was always the possibility they would end up online. You hear lots about that sort of thing."

"I guess love leads to trust. When you're at that stage in a relationship and you think you love someone, you just can't imagine them doing that."

"Was it love?"

"Thought so. At the time."

"And these photos. Were they—?"

"Explicit? Yes, Harold, they were."

"How did you feel when you saw the pictures on the internet?"

"Are you mad? How do you think I felt?"

Conversation halted when the main courses arrived, but when they'd finished eating, it was clear Hannah had more to say about her ex.

"Do you know, Harold, after we'd split up, and I was in a terrible dark place after those photos appeared, the bastard sent me a link to a mental health charity with a nasty little note suggesting my mind was as soft as my body and both needed sorting out."

Hannah spat out the last three words and cried.

Reaching for her across the table, Harold knocked over the wine glasses.

Hannah squealed, but a quick-thinking waiter stepped to the table and cleared the mess. Another replaced the wine.

Mindful they were once again the centre of attention, Harold asked, "Shall we change the subject?"

He relaxed as she nodded, tensing as she challenged.

"What do you think about women's bodies? Do you like them cuddly? Or lean and mean?"

For a third time, food intervened. Desserts and the sweet wine Hannah was keen to try.

"Harold, I'm enjoying all this. Thank you so much and I'm sorry if my behaviour embarrasses you. Sometimes, I embarrass myself."

Relieved the meal was ending, Harold said nothing, his smile tight. Tired, he looked forward to the quiet of his cabin with no more drama. It wasn't to be. Harold refused his liqueur but, before he could stop her, Hannah downed his as well as her own.

Slurring, she went off again. "More about that jerk. He was such a shit. Can't begin to tell you."

"So don't. We should leave."

It was clear Hannah was drunk. Giggling, she couldn't balance on her sandals, eyes blinking, trying to focus. Ignoring smirking waiters and curious diners, Harold placed his hand under her elbow. She made to resist.

"Let's go out onto the deck and you can tell me all about it there."

A few people strolled by, but the sound of the sea below and the stiff breeze convinced Harold that any noise Hannah made wouldn't carry.

On cue, and without prompting, Hannah yelled, "The bastard. He thought it was funny that I ended up sectioned. I was a complete wreck, and he made a joke of it. Wasn't enough to abuse my body, he had to abuse my mind as well."

Hannah wailed, head down, holding onto the edge of the deck, heaving breaths forcing their way from her quaking body punctuated with hysterical laughter. Tears swamped a face red and ugly in its grief. Watching in horror, then pity, Harold didn't know what to do. Just as he thought he should seek help, Hannah shuddered and took calming breaths.

"I'm getting cold. Can we go in now, please?"

Harold took Hannah's arm. She clung to him as they took the lift and made for the corridor leading to the cabins. He struggled for something to say.

At last he managed, "Cadiz tomorrow."

"Really? We haven't finished with today yet."

21

Harold's plan backfired. Instead of seeing Hannah to her cabin, saying goodnight, then retiring, he found himself pinned to the wall, mouth clamped by two probing red lips.

The experience was a new sensation and not without pleasure—excitement even—but alcohol breath and a sense of imprisonment put Harold off. As Hannah pressed him against the wall, his horror at the possibility of discovery in such an embarrassing situation overwhelmed him.

Finally pulling away for air, Hannah panted a triumphant, "Ha."

Harold's feeble protests fought rapid breathing. "I think it's time we went our separate ways."

"Oh, you do, do you? I want to find out where you stand on women's bodies."

"What do you mean?"

"I think you know what I mean."

"Well, I'm sorry, but I'm going to bed now."

"Yes, you are, Harold. With me."

Grabbing his belt, Hannah tugged Harold towards her cabin door. Stunned, he pulled away.

"I'm going to scream if you don't let me take you into my cabin."

"Hannah, please."

Harold looked to the end of the corridor and saw a couple heading towards them. The woman was in a wheelchair and for a horrible moment, he thought it was his mother. The distraction enabled Hannah to open the door and drag him inside.

"I just want some love."

She kissed him again, lowering her dress straps, then pulling off Harold's tie. She unbuttoned his shirt and pushed him back onto the bed. Making no effort to resist, he closed his eyes, part in embarrassment, part in a wave of alcohol-induced fatigue. He was aware of Hannah's body on top of his and her hand grasping the top of his trousers. Startled, his eyes flew open. The cabin spun. Struggling to breathe, a wave of heat passed through his body. He dragged himself from the bed and crawled into the bathroom, reaching the toilet just in time to throw up.

Slumped on the bathroom floor, legs splayed, back resting against the toilet, Harold's eyes opened to darkness. His head thumped, mouth tasted sour. His inclination was to go back to sleep, but he was desperate for water. Forcing himself to stand, Harold turned on the light, reached for a glass in the cabinet and gulped water. He staggered out of the bathroom and saw his clothes in a neat pile at the edge of the bed, presuming Hannah had put them there. There was no sign of her. Looking at the clock on her bedside table, it shocked him to see the time. Ignoring the vice-like grip around his head, he dressed and headed to his cabin, wincing as the corridor's bright lights hit him. He winced louder when entering.

"Good morning, sir. How are you today?" The stewardess greeted Harold with her usual broad smile and cheerful voice, assessing the state of him, then lowering her voice.

"I will leave you. Take your time. I will come back later."

* * *

After showering and brushing his teeth, Harold gulped two painkillers and viewed the CCTV image looking ahead from the ship's bridge. The picture showed clear blue sky and a section of a port. Cadiz. He switched channels and found the ship's information displaying current weather and forecast. Highest temperature: 24 degrees Celsius. When converted to Fahrenheit: mid-seventies. A pleasant day.

Dressed in casual summer wear, Harold contemplated a late breakfast but thought better of it. The appeal of strong black coffee beckoned, and he set off, first seeking much-needed fresh air and a circuit of walking around Deck 7. The open air and brilliant sunshine struck him as he stepped onto the deck and closed his eyes. When he opened them, he registered the stillness of the ship and the panorama of the port and city area. It surprised him to find only a handful of people on the deck. He'd expected more than he'd seen on his dawn walk, but remembered he was in Cadiz now and many passengers would be ashore sightseeing.

Harold went to the railings, looking at the quayside and beyond. A cluster of white buildings made up the historic Spanish port city, the most eye-catching being the 18th- century golden-domed cathedral. Dizzied for a moment, Harold didn't know which way to turn, gripped by a whirlpool of emotions, memories, and thoughts. The uplifting sight of Cadiz, sunshine, and bright blue sky offset the acute embarrassment and discomfort of last night. Screwing up his eyes, Harold attempted to recall details of last night.

What had happened between him and Hannah? Where was she now?

22

Harold didn't go into Cadiz. Humiliating memories of vomiting in Hannah's cabin, drunken fumbles, and a lingering hangover meant he couldn't summon the mental and physical energy to explore a foreign land.

It was easier to stay on board. Comfortable. Even the laziest of days passed quickly. After coffee, he went to the cyber suite, resisting the temptation to email Dorothy. Instead, he checked the local news websites just in case, but found nothing more concerning library cuts and rumours of a big lottery winner. He had time to go up onto the top deck and sketch the panoramic port scenery. He'd take photographs too.

Harold had been on the top deck a short while when activity around the gangplank distracted him. He saw a gathering, heard the buzz of voices, bursts of laughter. Lifting the camera, he zoomed to focus. Crew members bobbed up and down, hauling a collection of designer suitcases from the quay and carrying them on board. As they moved away, Harold saw a tall, distinguished man raise his white peaked cap and salute to someone in the distance. From the man's insignia and bearing, Harold recognised the ship's captain and wondered who he was waiting for.

Seconds later, a woman came into view. Even from a distance and through a lens, Harold could see she was captivating. Wearing a white one-piece jumpsuit with bold blue vertical stripes, a narrow belt cinching her in at the waist, the woman glided to the captain in high-heeled sandals. Off came her big sunhat, revealing a head of golden hair before flinging herself into the captain's outstretched arms.

Harold thought they made an attractive couple and wondered if a girl would ever fall into his arms. A memory of unfilled desire tugged but, tired and befuddled from last night's antics, he gave up trying to call it to mind and packed up.

Lunch came and went, with none of Harold's six companions showing. While the sun blazed outside, he chose the comfort of the cinema and fell asleep watching a film. The ship was due to sail at 5pm. Passengers knew punctuality was crucial—no waiting for stragglers. Not even Hannah, Harold thought with a wry smile. There'd be the usual sailaway party around the pool at the stern. Harold knew of one young lady who would attend. He always felt good in Angie's company and figured she may know of Hannah's whereabouts and what she'd been up to.

Angie was there, wrapped in a towel, and joined Harold at the poolside. "Where've you been all day?"

"Here and there. Nowhere special."

Harold's lacklustre response prompted Angie to work on lifting his mood. She launched into a refreshing account of her activities, enthusing about the open-top bus tour of historical sights and the delights of a beach she'd found, where she'd swam in clear seas. Her enthusiasm was infectious, and Harold found himself taking an interest not just in what she was saying, but in Angie herself.

He felt more at ease than at any time since he'd met up with Hannah ahead of their dinner last night. Angie had a balanced voice, easy on the ear. Taken with her welcoming manner, Harold found her company soothing and rather seductive, particularly when she asked when they would have their special dinner.

"Not tonight. Nor tomorrow."

Angie's face dropped. It wasn't the answer she'd expected, and she was hurt, puzzled.

"I don't want to go two nights running without joining everyone for dinner, and tomorrow is the captain's reception and gala dinner. It would be a shame to miss that. I thought you and I could go out together on Monday evening. After two more days at sea, it'll be a treat for us both."

Angie beamed, and Harold smiled back at her obvious pleasure. He noticed how her smile lit up her face and how pretty she looked, the start of a tan making her skin glow and highlighting sparkling eyes.

"Great idea. After Cadiz, I'm really looking forward to Malta after our two days at sea. Then, after another day's sailing, it's Venice, the highlight of the cruise. I can't wait."

Harold relaxed, warm in the glow of Angie's happiness, no longer inclined to raise the subject of Hannah. As if thinking had summoned her, he spotted Hannah walking on the other side of the pool. One hand carried a large cocktail, the other clasped in the hand of a tall, dark young man. Harold was sure the guy was a member of the ship's entertainment team, who performed in the theatre after dinner. Angie sensed his discomfort, but before she could speak, he stumbled to his feet.

"Sorry, I have to go. I'll see you at dinner tonight."

"Okay," Angie said, startled by the abrupt departure.

As he hurried to his cabin, Harold regretted rushing off. He'd been rude to Angie. He also felt foolish for not speaking to Hannah and knew he'd feel awkward at dinner. Harold felt no better for acknowledging that

Hannah was unlikely to have seen him, as she only had eyes for her companion. He threw himself on the bed, all pleasure from his poolside chat with Angie gone, recoiling from the memory of the last time he lay down on a bed.

His thoughts turned to Hannah and that man. *What is she up to with him?*

Ahead of dinner, Harold worked himself into a lather. Out of character, he needed a drink but didn't order when recalling where excessive alcohol landed him last night. He put off arriving for dinner as long as possible, standing in the entrance watching his lady companions chatting. Squaring his shoulders, he made his way to the table.

"Sorry, I'm late."

Breathless, Harold sat between Sandy and Angie and looked around. He had the impression they'd been talking about him as six voices greeted him with laughter and sly looks. To help his discomfort, he thought of asking how they'd spent their day, but Hannah spoke first.

"Remember that intro we did the other day, while we were waiting for you? I thought up a new version for tonight."

Harold tried not to panic.

"We'll go around the table, each of us giving our impression of the cruise so far and what we've been up to since boarding. In only two minutes. What do you think, Harold?"

"Fine, Hannah. If that's what you want."

"As it's my idea, I'll go last."

Harold strove to appear calm but scarcely noticed what he ate and only registered brief snatches of the conversation. Annette opened the discussion.

"Shore excursions are expensive."

"So much to do on board, and the food's great," gushed Debbie.

"I had a great session in the spa. Massage, the works," said Chloe.

Angie's grumble followed. "Don't like this idea of automatically adding tips to our account."

"I am enjoying very much. Thank you, Harold," said Sandy, polite and rather stiff as if she didn't understand what was being asked of her.

Then came the dreaded moment. Hannah took centre stage. She gave Harold a mad grin and his stomach dropped.

All theatre and show, Hannah threw out her arms. "I'm having a fabulous cruise. I love being waited on, love the entertainment, adore the cocktails, and I've met this incredible bloke."

As she spoke, Hannah stared at Harold. He stared back, wondering if she'd continue or leave him pondering. *Did she mean him or the man she was with at the pool?* He sensed the interest around the table, steeling himself to what was coming next.

"Last night, things came to a head when we ended up in bed, but it all ended in a horrible mess. I haven't seen him since, the bastard."

Harold frowned at Hannah's change of mood. There was an uneasy silence around the table until Annette cut in.

"Hannah, your two minutes are up. We've heard enough."

Harold's relief was tangible. "Thanks, Annette, and thank you, Hannah, and everyone else for sharing your thoughts. I'm glad you're enjoying yourselves. Time to call it a day."

"What, no showtime tonight?" Chloe said.

Avoiding Hannah's penetrating stare, Harold replied. "The meal has been enough for me tonight. Go ahead. I had an upset stomach last night and I'm still feeling a bit off. A quiet night for me. I'll see you tomorrow. Don't forget the captain's reception and gala dinner. Best dresses and best behaviour."

This time, Harold did not avert his gaze.

23

E mail from Harold to Dorothy:

Hello, Mum,

We've mostly been at sea apart from Cadiz on Saturday. Tomorrow, Valletta. I've seen no more news about the library, or the lottery win, but it's still a worry.

I'm having a one-to-one dinner with each of my companions to get to know them better. The first was with Hannah. She can be an embarrassment with her mood swings, and she knocks back the drink. I'm getting on okay with Annette, but don't think it will ever be more than that. You know I think the world of Sandy and I do like Angie. Think she likes me, too. She's my guest in the restaurant tonight, so I hope to get to know more about her.

Will send another update soon.

Love,

Harold x

24

Floating. The word in Harold's mind as he sat in the exclusive Azure restaurant. He'd experienced nothing like this. Post-Hannah, Harold was familiar with the routine. A bevy of attentive waiters, single rose on the table, soft lighting, extensive menu.

Sitting opposite, bathed in tantalizing, potent perfume, was the most beautiful woman Harold had ever been near. Resembling a 1950s film star, Angie was with him for the evening clad in a black silk dress, with boat neckline, long lace sleeves, full skirt. A black choker—gold heart in its centre—and dainty gold hooped earrings enhanced the image. Angie's tanned face wore minimal make-up. A lick of mascara, a drizzle of lip gloss.

"You look like a character from one of my favourite films. Tatiana Romanova wore a choker just like that in *From Russia with Love.*"

"Oh, dear. Does it look old-fashioned? I'll take it off if you like."

"No, it's perfect."

Harold couldn't believe the infinite contrast between tonight and his dinner with Hannah. More than anything, he was aware he felt relaxed and proud to be sharing a table with this lovely woman, contrary to his discomfort and embarrassment with the unpredictable Hannah. The composed, softly spoken Angie, her manner and its effect on him keeping Harold at ease when she slipped into the conversation the items of news that concerned him. He was happy to discuss the library issue, but on his guard when Angie was eager to discuss the possibility of a lottery winner in the Porthcoombe area.

"I mean, what would *you* do if you won the lottery? Would you want publicity or to stay anonymous?"

"Definitely anonymous," Harold said, knowing he must have appeared ready with his answer.

Angie smiled. "Reckon it would be impossible for a lottery winner to keep their identity secret in a small place like Porthcoombe, don't you?"

Harold nodded, somehow keeping his smile. He evaded shuffling around in his seat, while Angie maintained her embracing look. *Was it only a smile—the most natural thing on this special occasion—or a hint that she was onto him?*

Harold decided discretion or continued silence would not be the better of valour. "I imagine it's human instinct to want privacy with a life-changing event. Your first thought would be to maintain normality in your life, or maybe not. For instance, I'm not sure I'd want to give up my job as a librarian. I enjoy it too much."

"A life-changing event." Angie's look screamed speculation.

Harold swigged the last of his brandy. "Let's go for a walk out on deck."

Looking out to sea from the deck railings, the couple admired a spectacular sunset. A pleasant evening, not a breath of wind, the hiss of the wake below as the ship cruised the calm Mediterranean. Harold relaxed once more, taking in the vast panorama, warming to the feeling of Angie leaning against his side.

"Good to get away from it all." Harold didn't have time to regret his words.

Angie seized her chance to resume the table conversation. "I bet that's what the lottery winner would yearn for if they came under constant pressure to reveal their identity."

Harold said nothing, holding his gaze out to sea. "Can't beat peace and quiet."

"Oh, I can think of other things." Angie couldn't resist teasing.

Lost for words, he changed the subject. "What would you like to do next? It'll be time for the show soon."

"I'm not in the mood for the show tonight. I'd rather have a nightcap with you, please."

Harold didn't want more alcohol, but did want more time with Angie. He saw no point in resisting. Heading to one of the ship's bars, he sensed intense pleasure as Angie took his hand. Conflicting thoughts and emotions persisted. The simple act of Angie's hand in his produced a new feeling of warmth and excitement. but he couldn't imagine her being attracted to him. *If she was onto him, did she want him for money or was there another reason for her behaviour?*

To his dismay, Cowboy's warning came to mind, the image receding as he and Angie ordered drinks. Harold's concern over his choice of words disappeared when Debbie, Chloe, and Annette turned up.

"Hi. We saw you come in here and thought we'd join you for a quick chat," Chloe said.

The group talked a while, then Debbie said, "We'd better be on our way or we'll be late for the show. Are you joining us?"

"Think we'll give it a miss tonight," Angie said.

Chloe made to respond, but Debbie moved her and Annette on with a deft nudge.

"See you tomorrow." Chloe couldn't resist.

Paranoia mounted a fresh attack on Harold. Oh, Lord, now they'll be talking about Angie and me. Analysing every word, saying goodness knows behind our backs. Anxiety heightened when Angie leaned into him.

"Don't know about you, but I'm ready for bed."

As the couple walked to their cabins, tipsy Angie clung to Harold, making a blatant return to the topic he hoped had died.

"Harold, supposing you *were* the lottery winner and the press *was* onto you. Wouldn't it be better to give a story and have done with it? Just to one reporter? You know, what they call an exclusive."

Staying silent, Harold quickened his pace.

"It couldn't be cheque book journalism in your case, because you'd already have too much of the stuff, wouldn't you? Money, I mean, as in vast fortune." Angie chuckled.

Harold's lips stayed sealed as they reached Angie's cabin.

"But, if there was something else on offer, I reckon it might tempt you, hmm?" A dreamy look into Harold's eyes.

"I can't think what you have in mind."

"Oh, I think you do." Angie's tone challenged.

"Goodnight, Angie. Thanks for a lovely evening." Harold drew her face to his for a goodnight kiss.

Angie was in no mood for a hasty parting. She put her arm around Harold's waist and drew him towards her.

"Would you like to see my cabin?"

He made to move away, but Angie pulled him back. "It's been such a lovely evening. I don't want it to end with you just walking away."

She lifted her face to Harold and kissed him, rendering him helpless. Before he knew it, they were in her cabin and she was loosening his tie, unbuttoning his shirt. Pulling down the straps of her dress, she let it fall to the floor.

Pressing herself against him, she whispered, "Come on. Time for bed, and I don't mean sleep!"

* * *

Harold woke hours later. Although dazed, he knew he wasn't in his own cabin but was wide awake when he grasped he wasn't alone.

Sleeping on her side, hands tucked under her cheek, Angie's bare shoulders peeked from under the bedclothes. Harold panicked, remembering the disastrous finale to his dinner date last night.

'Let's try again in the morning,' she'd said.

Fear of another failure drove Harold out of bed and back into the crumpled dinner suit lying in a heap on the floor. Desperate for air, he let himself out, pacing the deck, reliving his humiliating bedroom bungle. As the sun rose, passengers walked or jogged before breakfast. Looking askance at Harold's bizarre attire and dishevelled appearance, he realised there was a danger of Sandy spotting him on her daily run. How mortifying.

Dejected, Harold couldn't face Angie and escaped to his cabin. He leaned against the door and hung his head. Finding a girlfriend, let alone a wife, was proving an impossible challenge.

25

H i, Roy,

Harold hasn't admitted to being the lottery winner, and I didn't ask outright, but did ask a few questions. His replies convinced me it's him.

Do you want a speculative piece in the meantime?

Angie

* * *

Hello, Mum,

You haven't replied to my last email, but I'm worried about something. Angie's asking me questions about the lottery winner and I think she may be a reporter.

Also, Sandy got upset when I said she must be looking forward to revisiting Croatia. Do you know why?

Harold x

ps No further incidents concerning Hannah, who seems to have got in with the ship's entertainment company.

* * *

Hi, Angie,

Good news about your progress, but you need to be careful with this. Have a bash with the speculative piece and email me for consideration.

Regards.

Roy

* * *

Dear Harold,

Angie could be behind that nasty little story in the *Clarion*. Be firm and remind her of the terms of the cruise. No questions asked.

As for Sandy, it's for her to tell you whatever and whenever she wants. It's painful territory for her. Sensitivity needed.

Love,

Mum x

26

The gondolier assured Harold the boat could accommodate the group. Though she'd said she would come along, Hannah didn't. Accustomed to her changeable behaviour, her no-show didn't bother Harold.

The *Gem of the Seas*, one of five giant vessels berthed at Venice's cruise ship terminal, dominated the skyline for miles around. Achieved with impressive speed and efficiency, ship's staff had the mass evacuation of passengers honed down to a fine art. A fleet of tenders took droves down the lagoon to the city hub.

Perching in the gondola's stern and in danger of falling overboard, Angie posed with the others for a challenging selfie. In obligatory black trousers, striped shirt, and straw hat, the gondolier waited, single oar at the ready, face nailed in a bored expression.

Angie snapped with her camera. "Reckon there's one or two good ones among that lot, and here's the perfect caption kick-start. Fanfare, folks. Harold's Harem. Ta-da."

The women giggled. Harold's face dropped. Cigarette stuck between his lips, gondolier man remained impassive. Harold signalled the journey could start. With a forced smile and quiet tone, he collared Angie.

"I'd like a word with you later, please."

Intent on not spoiling the mood, Angie replied in mock fear. "Ooh. Don't like the sound of that."

As the gondola glided away, Harold knew now was not the time for that word. Heading for the heart of the city, he relaxed in comfort on the beautiful hand-painted boat, smiling at the ladies' wows and whoops as they navigated canals, sailed under stone bridges, and passed balconied waterfront buildings. In places, the canals were so narrow, one believed they could reach out and touch high-rise buildings on either side.

After leaving the gondola, St Mark's Square beckoned, strolling among hundreds of pigeons and thousands of people, marvelling at impressive sights. St Mark's Basilica—gold mosaic arches, five domes, and, overlooking the city, the Basilica's prominent bell tower, 300ft tall Campanile San Marco.

At a table in an archway bordering the square, the group listened to the musicians and opted for coffee. They were about to sit down when a man barged in front, his camera aimed at the menu on the table.

"Excuse me, I must take a photo of this or the folks back home will never believe me. I mean, fourteen euros for a cup of coffee. Can you believe it?"

Harold looked at the menu. Yes, the man was right, but cost wasn't a worry. To the pushy tourist's astonishment, an exuberant Harold gestured to his friends. "Take a seat, ladies. We'll have coffee here."

Savouring the moment, the women sat down.

Harold joined them, "I bet the coffee's a fraction of the price around the corner, but you can't put a price on the ambience here and the orchestra is wonderful."

As the rest of the group chatted about the day so far, Harold took Angie to one side. "About that photo on the gondola."

"Yes?"

"Two things. First, I'm not sure about Harold's Harem."

Angie laughed. "I thought that would be a fantastic title for your book."

"As it's my book, I hope I've the right to approve the title, and I don't want that one."

"Okay. What's the second thing?"

"You said Harold's Harem would make a good caption kick-start or something. What's that?"

"A term used for the start of a photo caption reflecting what people see and detailing what the caption goes on to say. It kick-starts the caption. Pick up any newspaper and you'll see what I mean."

"Seems you know a lot about newspaper goings-on."

Harold studied Angie's reaction, noting her momentary struggle and loss of smile.

"Newspapers, books, same thing. You'll see many examples of caption kickstarts in books. I meant books, Harold."

Harold's stare persisted, but his voice was soft. "Angie, may I ask a straight question?"

Unable to hide her discomfort, Angie shuffled in her chair. "Go on."

"Are you who you say you are, or a journalist with the *Cornwall Clarion?*"

Shocked, her mouth flew open, but Harold ploughed on.

"Was it you who gave that piece about the lottery winner?"

Angie looked pained, and Harold was sure her eyes watered.

At last she spoke in a firm, even tone. "No. Hand on heart, swear to God, whatever you want. The answer is no on both counts, and I'm sorry you think that of me, Harold."

Either she's a first-class actress or I've hurt her feelings and blown my friendship with her.

"Okay, that's good enough for me. I'm sorry."

Harold clasped Angie's hand, unaware the others gawked.

"What's that all about?" Annette asked.

"Nothing." Angie lowered her head.

Leaving the women combing rows of market stalls, Harold hatched a plan.

27

H i, Roy,

Think it's best holding off with that piece I had in mind. I'll keep you posted.

Regards.

Angie

* * *

Hello, Mum,

I asked Angie whether she was working for the *Cornwall Clarion* and she denied it, but I still doubt her. I've mentioned it to the others too and wonder if this will flush her out?

Love,

Harold x

Dear Harold,

After getting your email, I phoned the *Clarion a*nd asked to speak to Angie Swan. I was told they didn't have anyone with that name. She wasn't responsible for that story, so forget it.

Enjoy tonight's dinner with Sandy.

Love,

Mum x

28

In the Azure restaurant, before helping to slip a soft shawl across Sandy's slim shoulders, Harold admired the stunning impact of her midnight blue, floor-length fishtail evening gown. Fashioned with demure crossover neckline and dramatic, plunging back, the revelation Sandy designed the dress using budget material from a local market back home made the creation more striking. Harold's astonishment had prompted a proud Sandy to explain that making clothes was second nature to many women in her native Croatia.

From childhood, there was an expectation Sandy would become proficient in traditional home skills, and the gown she wore confirmed her gift as a seamstress. Her previous career, to which she was about to allude, had given her a taste of making the best of herself. Harold's incredulity soared on learning Sandy's glittering blue earrings and necklace were made of glass and matching blue satin shoes were white satin cast-offs, dyed to complement her dress.

"I want to tell you something, Harold, but not here with other people around. I have a good place. Can we go to the back of the ship, on the pool deck?"

"Of course."

The couple thanked the waiters and maître d' and headed into the main corridor, thronging with passengers on their way to the late-night show. Passing crowded bars and casinos, Harold and Sandy headed in the opposite direction. It was another balmy evening in the waning moments of dusk. Hitting the night air at the ship's stern, the couple decided they didn't need to cover up, hanging Sandy's shawl and Harold's jacket on a sun lounger.

A few hours earlier, everyone had marvelled at the stunning views as the towering *Gem of the Seas* steamed down through the Venice lagoon, the city's breathtaking array of grand palaces and churches spread out below on either side of the waterway. The vessel was now out into the Adriatic, bound for the Croatian port of Korcula. The open-air swimming pool and jacuzzi spas were under cover for the night and the couple were alone, save for occasional lovers who moved on when seeing another pair bagging the romantic spot. Harold and Sandy leaned against the railings at the end of the ship beneath two giant controllable pitch propellers, which created a phenomenal hissing wake of white froth visible in the black mass of surrounding sea.

Soft lighting illuminated the deck, giving Harold the chance of intimacy he wanted. He'd long expected that he would find it difficult—one of those 'lines that shouldn't be crossed' moments. Still, in semi-darkness, and with nothing else but water for company, putting his arm around Sandy and drawing her to him was the easiest thing to do. She offered no resistance, her head resting against his shoulder as they gazed seawards, neither speaking during those precious moments.

In time, Harold ventured close to whisper in her ear. "You said you wanted to tell me something."

Sandy remained silent, but it relieved Harold to see she nodded her head. "I will tell you. Just once. Tell you why I will not go ashore into Croatia tomorrow, but when I tell you, no questions. I don't want to talk about it ever again."

Harold said nothing.

Still looking ahead, Sandy spoke. "Do we have, how do you call it, a deal?"

Harold squeezed her. "Of course, Sandy. We have a deal."

Relaxing his grip, Harold waited. The next sound when it came was not a word but a sniffle. Alarmed, he saw Sandy struggling to hold back tears, prompting him to speak.

"It's okay, Sandy. If you'd rather not, please don't. It can wait, or you don't need to tell me at all."

"No, no, I want." Taking a handkerchief from her bag, Sandy dabbed her eyes, blew her nose.

Overwhelmed with an all-consuming desire to pick up his beloved Sandy, cradle her in his arms and wrap her in love, Harold experienced the depth of feeling one human can have for another. A first-time feeling.

"Okay. I came to the UK as a refugee when I was seventeen. You know about Balkan wars, of course. Or rather the last one in nineteen ninety-one."

"Yes."

"I lost my mother and two of my brothers in that war."

Harold's hold tightened.

"I was just a child then. It's a long story, as you say, but when I grew into my teens I became, what you call, a human trafficking victim. A sex slave. I was beaten, raped again and again, forced to be prosti—"

Sandy stumbled over the word. Disturbed, Harold had an urge to put his hand across her mouth.

A wolf whistle and cry of, "Night-night, lovebirds," shattered the moment.

Harold turned to look at the shadow of a staggering couple on the other side of the swimming pool. The woman hushed the man, pulling him back towards the crowds inside.

Sandy didn't move, but made a sound that Harold couldn't make out. Was she crying or laughing? He concluded a combination of both, continuing to hold her, not knowing what to say. On reflection, silence was the best option for the time being. If he was honest, he didn't want to hear more.

As if reading his thoughts, Sandy spoke. "I think I have told you enough and think you understand now why I will not go back into Croatia tomorrow. I cannot—too many bad memories."

"I understand."

"You will go tomorrow? To Korcula?"

"Yes. I've booked a shore excursion, the scenic tour. What will you do?"

"Don't worry about me, Harold. I will stay on the ship. I will be okay."

Arm in arm, they turned and headed back into the heart of the liner, reaching the long corridor leading down to their cabins.

"I have been so happy since I came to the UK. Years of looking after your mother have been the happiest of my life. She is kind to me. I love her. I love you." Sandy smiled.

Harold wanted to say, 'I love you, too,' but was unsure how much value to place on her use of the love word. He had a half-forgotten memory from school that in many languages like and love were the same thing.

While pondering, Sandy's smile vanished and her tone changed. "Harold, do you think bad of me?"

Harold hugged her so tight and for so long that she squeaked.

"I think that's your answer."

Sandy lifted her face and looked through damp eyelashes into Harold's eyes. He reached out, tracing the side of her face with infinite softness before planting a gentle kiss on her forehead.

"Thank you and thank you for tonight. For a lovely meal, for listening, understanding."

They kissed, tentatively at first, lips brushing, then urgent, passionate, leaving them both breathless.

Sandy stopped and pulled away, eyes shining with pleasure.

"Good night, Harold."

"Good night. I'll see you tomorrow."

"Yes."

With that, she was gone.

29

Harold replayed Sandy's use of the love word, deciding how significant that choice had been. Until putting out his nightlight, the warmth and softness of her lips and smell of perfume lingered. The fragrance of Sandy's long, dark hair and feel of her body pressed against his stirred sensations that had slept for too long.

Next morning, Harold showered, shaved, and took to the top deck, hoping to see Sandy on her dawn run. The scenery stunned, the towering coastline on either side suggesting a smaller version of the Norwegian fjords, as the *Gem of the Seas* glided towards the medieval Dalmatian town of Korcula. The one image Harold wanted to see more than any other wasn't there. Sandy didn't show.

He walked several circuits of the deck, longing for her to appear, but to no avail, and moved on for breakfast at the buffet restaurant overlooking the pool area where he and Sandy shared intimate moments last night. Harold stalled over breakfast, made his pot of tea last longer, but still, no Sandy. He stayed for two hours beside the enormous windows looking down at the sea. Oblivious to the restaurant filling up with passengers, he gazed ashore to the distinctive rust-red roofs of Korcula. Too small to accommodate a large cruise ship, the *Gem of the Seas* anchored a mile offshore, a shuttle service of tenders ferrying from ship to quayside and back throughout the day.

The restaurant emptied once more, as did the ship, most of the cruisers choosing to go ashore. Harold looked at his watch: 10:08. Breakfast service stopped at ten-thirty. Surely, Sandy wouldn't miss it. At last, he saw her before she spotted him. He stood. Apprehensive, then breaking into a broad smile, Sandy made for his table. Harold gestured her to sit down. She wore a tracksuit, hair tied up, and Harold saw a film of perspiration around her neck. Damp hair stuck to her forehead. She must have been for her run, after all.

Both spoke at the same time.

Harold raised his hands. "You first."

"I wasn't expecting to see you here."

Unable to stop himself, Harold said, "I hope you're not sorry."

Sandy's scolding teased. "No, Harold, I am not sorry, but you should be on land by now. You'll miss your excursion."

"I've already missed it, and you aren't the only one who's not feeling sorry right now."

Saying nothing, her smile was warm.

"Have you come up for breakfast or mid-morning coffee?"

"Breakfast."

"I'd better let you go before they stop serving. Do you mind if I stay and chat for a while?"

"I would like that very much."

Sandy went to the food counters, returning with a tray of fruit juice, pastries, and a banana. The couple said little as she ate.

Before long, Harold asked the inevitable question. "What will you do today?"

"After breakfast, I must have a shower."

"No, I mean the rest of the day. There's time to kill before the ship sails at six."

Sandy frowned then shrugged. "I will find things to do."

Nothing ventured. "Sandy, can I make a suggestion?"

"Yes, but I think I know what you want to say and I think you know my answer."

Harold smiled and reached across the table to take her hand. "Let me take you ashore."

Looking down, she shook her head.

Putting his finger beneath her chin, Harold tilted Sandy's face to look outside. She had tears in her eyes. "Look, it's a wonderful day. Brilliant sunshine, gorgeous, calm sea, and a beautiful little town just waiting for us. Let's go over in the tender together and walk along the waterfront. The moment you've had enough, we can come back. I promise."

Harold knew what he proposed to say next was selfish and bordering on emotional blackmail, but went ahead anyway. "Sandy, I'd be privileged to take you back to your homeland. How about it?"

Still, she said nothing, her head remaining low. To Harold's discomfort, he realised she was sobbing. He squeezed her hand and offered a paper napkin to wipe her face.

The crying bought him time to think. When she'd composed herself, he spoke, voice soft. "Okay, Sandy, here's a suggestion. Have your shower, then if the answer's yes, meet me here in an hour. We'll go ashore and have a coffee together first to ease the nerves. I'll be waiting for you."

Sandy offered a brave smile. "Okay, Harold, that is a good idea, but please, still think good of me if I do not come."

"Of course."

30

In a pretty blue T-shirt, white shorts, and sandals, Sandy met Harold. She wore sunglasses, blue-ribboned straw sun hat and a brave smile. He wore shorts and a burning heart.

The couple went down to Deck 4, boarding the tender bobbing alongside the vast hull of the ship, and sat together, looking out at the idyllic scene. Glittering, calm sea all around, glorious, towering coastal scenery, and his sweetheart's arm resting against his. Harold had never felt happier. In a short time, he helped Sandy from the foot of the steps leading up to the quayside and they set off towards the shops and cafés. He didn't remove his hand; Sandy's felt good wrapped in his.

"Would you like that coffee first?" he asked, sensing her misgivings in returning to her native land.

"Yes, please."

The couple navigated a steep, narrow lane to find a table, arching branches of nearby trees framing a breathtaking view of the harbour, the *Gem of the Seas* in the distance, the coastal stretches on either side.

A waitress took their order, her smile breathing warmth and cheer.

"Orange juice, please, it's so warm," said Sandy.

Harold opted for coffee.

Other than admiring the scenery, the pair said little, Harold knowing the only sensible course was to leave Sandy to speak in her own time.

After finishing their drinks, he asked, "What next? Shops and stalls, maybe, buy one or two souvenirs? Or a look at the medieval towers and walls, or the cathedral?"

A vigorous shake of the head and a forced smile. "No, thank you." A walk beside the water, please."

"I'd like that."

Hand in hand, they strolled along the cobblestones, passing stalls, saying nothing. Instead of heading inwards to the shops, they made for the west to the waterside walk. A strip of beach below and aromatic plants above provided welcome shade. Alien to such heat, Harold wilted. Sensing his discomfort, Sandy steered him to a wooden seat under a fig tree. He put his arm around her but no words passed, while gazing across the water at tenders ferrying backwards and forwards between the cruise ship and quayside.

Silence reigned, but Harold could see Sandy had relaxed, his relief tangible. Her body had loosened and she no longer fought tears. Harold had nothing useful to say. Better to leave her alone with her thoughts for as long as she needed. When the silence became uncomfortable, he had to break it.

"Sandy, can I say something? I'm no counsellor, but … do you know what a counsellor is?"

"Local politics?"

"Not exactly, but no matter. The thing is, there are therapies, treatments."

She frowned.

Harold went on. "You know about psychology. There are many treatments that could help you come to terms with your memories, live with them, help you love your homeland once more. If you'd like to find out more about such therapy, whatever it takes, I'll pay. The full cost, everything involved."

Harold feared Sandy would never reply. At last, she spoke. "Thank you. Maybe."

"There's also such a thing as art therapy. Expressing yourself, addressing problems through painting. I could help you with that, at least on the practical side. You may use my materials whenever you wish."

Sandy frowned again. "Okay, perhaps. That is kind, but enough for now. I have enjoyed today. Thank you, Harold, thank you for bringing me here."

She smiled, raised her head, and kissed him on the lips.

"Saw that."

Chloe's triumphant cry from behind startled Sandy, who tried to pull away. Harold hugged her tighter, sensing the tension in her body before they both turned around to see Chloe, Angie, and Debbie a few yards away. Even in his reverie, Harold was sharp enough to notice Chloe and Debbie's genuine smiles and Angie's hurt look hinting at a smile. The women stayed to chat awhile before returning to the ship.

"I would like to go back now, too."

Harold looked at his watch. "I thought we'd be back in time for lunch, but we're too late. Maybe afternoon tea?"

"I would like some time on my own when we get back to, how you say, afflect on this morning." Sandy hoped she hadn't offended Harold.

"Reflect."

"Yes. Reflect."

Ahead, Angie, Debbie, and Chloe stopped to let the couple catch up.

"It's a shame we didn't bring our swimming costumes. We could have swum in the sea. Maybe the pool when we get back on the ship?"

"No, thank you. I will see you tonight at dinner."

At this, Angie edged closer to Harold. "I'd love a swim. I'll join you in the pool if you like."

With Sandy consuming his thoughts, Harold felt inclined to say no, but couldn't find a way without appearing rude.

"Okay."

Angie pretended not to notice his lack of enthusiasm. "Great. Besides, I want a word with you."

31

After swimming, Angie and Harold relaxed on sun loungers beside the pool.

"I'm worried about Hannah's strange behaviour, Harold. Don't know what she's told you, but I suspect you don't know the full story."

Unable to let go of his suspicions about her, Harold registered Angie's use of 'full story.'

"Haven't seen much of Hannah these last few days, haven't had a proper chat with her. I'm not sure I'd know what to say. What full story?"

Angie lowered her voice. "She's in a relationship of sorts with one of the entertainment team. By the sound of it, he's not treating her right, and she strikes me as being mixed up."

A waitress interrupted their conversation and Harold ordered two cocktails.

Angie continued the conversation. "Apparently, this guy found some stuff on the internet. You know, Hannah's porn victim bits posted by her ex, the photos of her in the nude and so on."

"Lord, no."

"Yes. I thought they'd all gone, but there are some still out there putting Hannah on a massive downer. The guy keeps calling her his porn star."

"I thought there'd be rules, a policy prohibiting passenger-crew relationships. Maybe it's not the same for the entertainment company. They'll be on contract, freelance or whatever, won't they?"

"Not sure, but this guy thinks it's all a big laugh and is threatening to share with his pals. Hannah can't tell if he's joking or serious. She's looked at what's still on social media, reminding her of the insults and abuse. She's in a bad place right now."

Harold shook his head. "I'll have to think about this. Chances are I won't see her tonight as I've already booked dinner with Chloe."

Harold found Angie's smile and pout hard to read. *A hint of jealously, perhaps?*

"That sun's intense, isn't it? We should put some lotion on." Lowering her lounger, Angie turned onto her front, unhooked her bikini top, and waved the bottle at Harold. "Would you rub some on my back, please?"

Arrival of the drinks saved Harold from doing or saying anything. He was taking no chances and remained lying down, only for apprehension to grip once more, when Angie propped herself up and turned to him.

"That wasn't the only word I wanted to have with you."

Harold's instinct told him he wouldn't enjoy what was to come."

"Go on."

"I wanted to make sure that we are still friends. Are we?"

"Yes. Why shouldn't we be?"

"Oh, come on. You know what I mean. After the other night."

"Yes, of course we're still friends, but—"

"Shh. It's okay. I know you fancy Sandy, don't you?"

Harold paused. "Yes. Yes, I do."

"I can tell."

Harold relaxed, going back on his guard when Angie resumed. "As we're in the mood for trading confidences."

"Are we?"

"Well, you've confessed your love for Sandy. You remember a conversation we had when you asked if I was a reporter working for the *Cornwall Clarion*?"

"Yes."

"And I convinced you I wasn't."

Harold nodded.

"Now it's your turn."

"What do you mean?"

"I'm going to ask you a question and you're going to answer with the same assurance."

Rattled and unwilling to look her way, Harold rolled onto his front. Angie saw this as an opportunity to rub sun lotion on his back and legs. He tensed at the unexpected boldness, aware that Angie was sitting up, topless. Not knowing where to look, he screwed his eyes shut, but not for long. Her next words had a tsunami effect.

"You are the lottery winner, aren't you? Can you deny it, hand on heart, swearing to who or whatever is most dear to you?"

Harold's breath steadied. He turned over and looked into Angie's eyes.

"And you are a reporter, but not with the *Cornwall Clarion*."

Harold felt triumphant at the disbelief in Angie's face. Dropping her gaze, she grabbed her bikini top and collapsed onto the sun lounger. Fumbling to fasten the hooks, she lifted her face. Harold saw defeat, tears.

"Guess that's touché."

Shaken now, rather than pleased with confirming his suspicions, Harold remained firm. "Let me remind you of the terms of this cruise and the no questions clause. No questions of me, that is. There was nothing about me not questioning you. It's clear you're here under false pretences, and I have the right to ask."

Angie looked troubled. "Okay. I'll fess up. There's a lot to tell. I want to get it off my chest, but not here. Too public."

Inside the Blue Lagoon Bar, Angie told her story.

"I don't know whether you can forgive me, Harold, but I won't try to expose you. Whatever you think of me, I couldn't do that. Not now. It's obvious you don't want to be named as the lottery winner and I won't do that to you. I like you too much. There, I've said it, and I've seen how much you love Sandy. I don't want to do anything to spoil your happiness. That's the truth."

Harold relaxed, managing a weak smile as the bartender placed drinks and a plate of nibbles on their table.

"What about your job, your editor back at the *Gazette*? The story you hoped to get?"

"Don't worry. I'll get around that somehow. May even tell him a fib. Say I don't think it's you after all. Thing is, I can tell Roy's never been comfortable with the idea of me exposing you. I'm here in my own time, an open thing. I'm not obliged to get a story."

Harold wasn't convinced. "But surely this won't do your position any favours, will it? You're a trainee. You did such a hard-sell to your editor, feeding him emails, giving him every reason to believe you'd produce a sensational exclusive."

"It's one thing to conceive something and contemplate a great exposé, but quite another when you get to know and like the person concerned, as I've done with you."

Harold took Angie's hand.

"I'm wondering if I want to be a journalist after all, so, you've done me a favour in a way."

Angie hadn't convinced Harold of that either. "That's a bit dramatic. What would you do instead?"

"I'm enjoying this photography and book business. I may have a stab for real."

"What, and give up your job at the *Gazette*? There're a lot of photographers around, you know. Dozens graduate from Falmouth University every year. Could you make a living out of doing that?"

"I'd have the books, biographies also if I could make a success of that. I might even try my hand at PR, but I guess I'd have to take a course first."

"I'm sure there are plenty of courses available. I could help you with the funding."

"Oh, my God, you're really not too annoyed with me." More tears.

"Well, despite everything, I can't deny that I like you too and it took guts to fess up, as you say. Besides, it's possible you could help me with something."

32

Hello, Mum,

The big news is, Chloe's leaving. She confessed over dinner last night that she's flying home. It was a big shock, but it turns out Chloe and her late husband were seasoned cruisers and she can't handle being back on a liner without him.

You don't have to worry about Angie anymore, but it's a long story and must wait until I get home.

I'm still concerned about Hannah. She's got herself mixed up with a member of the entertainment crew and some of those nasty internet photos have resurfaced. I don't want to see her getting hurt again.

Love,

Harold x

33

While Sandy swam in the turquoise sea off Paleokastritsa, Harold floated on his back in a state of bliss. He had never known such happiness. The warm waves lapping his body made merciless sun rays bearable, the coastline shimmering in the heat, giving olive trees and white sugar-cube houses the appearance of a mirage. Mixed with the tang of ozone, a faint, sensual scent of jasmine from coastal gardens floated on the gentle breeze.

Bobbing in the water, Sandy laughed at shoals of fish swimming between her legs. Harold watched her against the dazzling light. Glowing skin, sparkling eyes, and wet hair moulded to her neck and shoulders reminded him of a water nymph. Catching him gazing, Sandy charmed Harold with a bewitching giggle.

Swimming and lazing in the sun, the happy couple watched the day drift away. Back on board, they enjoyed the show, then dinner with the rest of the party, minus Chloe and Hannah. As the *Gem of the Seas* steamed south, with Corfu behind and Messina ahead, they strolled on deck. Many other couples were out, enjoying the pleasant evening. Not wanting company, Harold and Sandy headed indoors.

Approaching their cabins, Sandy leaned her cheek against Harold's shoulder. "You remember when a man called out lovebirds that time? I think we are now, yes?"

"Yes, I think we are."

Harold snuggled Sandy against him and nuzzled her neck. She smelled of soap and shampoo, her delicious wholesomeness driving him to kiss her lips. He unlocked his cabin and led Sandy in, cupping her face in his hands, looking at her with abandoned desire.

"I love you, Sandy, and want you so much. I've never felt like this before. Until I met you, I didn't know it was possible to feel this way. I want to spend the rest of my time making you happy. I know life hasn't been easy for you."

Terrified he'd say the wrong thing and spoil the moment, Harold hesitated. Silent, but smiling, Sandy reached up and put her finger to his lips, then with infinite gentleness, unloosened his tie. She eased Harold's jacket from his shoulders before deft fingers undid his shirt buttons.

Touching Harold's belt, Sandy gazed at him, whispering the question. "You want?"

"Oh, yes, Sandy. I want."

Hours later, Harold woke from a deep sleep. Smiling, he came to, the fragrance of Sandy's hair dancing in the air, the delightful realisation she lay in his arms. The bedside clock showed 6:30am. Harold wanted to pinch himself. He'd spent the night with his new love and now heard the loveliest music—Sandy's steady breathing.

"I love you," he whispered.

"I love you, too."

Laughing, Harold kissed the top of Sandy's head before rolling her under him. Hours passed before they woke again.

Sandy was up first, surprising Harold by climbing out of bed and dressing.

"Hey, what are you doing? Stay a bit longer."

"I must go for my run."

"Surely not."

"Yes. I must keep fit."

An announcement boomed in the outside corridor.

"Can you tell what it's saying?" Sandy asked.

"Something about approaching Messina but slowing down first to lower lifeboats for sea trials and exercises today. We'll be going slow on the way out tonight while they lift the boats back. Nothing important."

Harold reached out to pull Sandy towards him.

She giggled. "No. I must run. Maybe more tonight, yes?"

"Definitely more tonight but I want to talk to you about something."

Sandy went to him and planted a kiss on his head. "After all this loving, my darling, I have no brain for thinking and talking. I need to run to wake up. See you at breakfast and we talk then."

"You win. Don't wear yourself out, save some energy for me."

With a cheeky wink, Sandy left the cabin. Harold flopped back onto the bed and closed his eyes, dreamy thoughts of the last few hours lulling him into a deep sleep.

34

The blissful day following the blissful night shattered at 18:07.

Breakfasting late, Harold and Sandy spent a few hours in Messina, the penultimate port on their cruise. Joining the crowds thronging the central square, they'd marvelled at the novelty of statues coming alive with sound and motion, then boarded an open-top double-decker bus for a tour of the historic harbour city. On the fringe of his and Sandy's bubble, people and panoramic views were secondary to Harold. Sights and sounds faded as his senses homed in on the woman beside him.

On returning to the ship, the couple swam, visiting the library before the voyage resumed. Free from machines, computers, and games, Harold welcomed the silence and presence of books, sharing with Sandy his concern for the future of public library services back home.

Back on deck, the couple waved goodbye to diminishing Messina as the *Gem of the Seas* headed out, slowing to lift lifeboats back into place after spending the day at sea for trials and exercises. The recovery operation attracted a crowd of spectators to the starboard side. While the rest circled in the calm, a pair of davits raised the first lifeboat from the water. In his peripheral vision, Harold noticed the daily quiz in the adjacent bar had attracted only a handful of participants, the ever-keen Annette among them.

The door to the corridor separating the outside deck and bar flung open, and all heads turned to a woman's panicked shriek.

"Help. Help! Man overboard. She's jumped in and can't swim."

A flurry of activity followed. Crew members communicated on walkie-talkies, and the ship's whistle sounded three deafening blasts as the standard Man Overboard drill swung into action. A horde of passengers—Harold and Sandy among them—made for the port side, rushing through the empty bar, unfinished quiz papers flying off tables in their wake. The crowd made it to the railings for a clear view of the drama unfolding below.

A head bobbed in the water, arms thrashing, face submerging and resurfacing, hair straggled over eyes. Far from recognisable, the sight was enough to horrify Harold.

"Oh, no. Dear God, no. I think that's Hannah."

"It is. I'm bloody sure of it." A familiar voice sounded to the left.

Harold turned to see Annette, who'd removed her shoes and stripped to her T-shirt and underwear. She climbed to the top of the railings and prepared to dive into the sea.

"No, no, Miss, you must not." The crew member insisted.

"It's okay. I know what I'm doing."

Before the man's outstretched hand could reach her, Annette was gone.

Among those who'd reached the railings was Angie Swan. Camera snapping, she caught Annette executing a textbook dive, itself bringing gasps of admiration from the crowd. Angie's zoom lens recorded the pair merging as Annette swam behind Hannah, manoeuvring to keep her head above water. While the camera rolled, Annette and Hannah grabbed a hurled lifebuoy, and a senior crew member activated a flare.

Angie photographed the unfolding drama as a ship's lifeboat arrived, diverting from its task on the other side of the liner. With Annette's help, crew members hauled a lifeless Hannah on board before pulling Annette from the water. Wrapped in blankets, the crew placed Hannah on a stretcher to perform CPR. After several tense minutes, she vomited amid a collective sigh of relief. The spectators flocked towards their original viewing area on the starboard side to watch a stricken Hannah brought back on board, where the stretcher party whisked her away to the ship's hospital on Deck 4.

Within two hours, the ship sailed well out to sea, once more steaming at 20 knots. Hannah was in the open air again, this time she and her carers on Deck 12, the roped-off tennis area performing its reserve role as a helipad. As Hannah's cruise host, Harold liaised with the ship's purser to assist with the formalities of transferring her to a mainland hospital in Messina. Before the air ambulance landed, Harold said a farewell to a drowsy, but conscious and stable Hannah.

In response, Hannah forced a grin. "They're coming to take me away, ha ha."

Harold grinned at the title of a 1960s novelty song that had become a worldwide hit. He kissed Hannah on the cheek. "I hope you'll find life can be beautiful."

For their own comfort and safety, staff asked Harold and Sandy to leave the landing area and return inside to avoid downdraft from the helicopter's landing. The couple left, feeling relieved and relaxed in the warmth of the ship's interior. It was too late for formal dinner, so they went up to the Roses buffet restaurant. After the night show, Harold surprised Sandy, saying he was wide awake and not yet ready for bed.

"I'm all wound up after tonight's events and it'll take ages getting to sleep. I'm going to send Mum an email. The latest news is too big to wait until tomorrow. Go up and I'll see you soon."

Harold guided Sandy to his cabin, let her in with his cruise card, then made for the cyber suite.

Dear Mum,

Hannah tried to commit suicide today by jumping into the sea. Annette dived in and saved her. A helicopter took Hannah to a Messina hospital and her father's flying out to take her home when she's discharged. It's shocking, and so soon after the upset of Chloe's departure.

This cruise is turning out to be even more memorable than we could have imagined!

Love,

Harold x

Still uptight, Harold looked at a couple of news websites. First, he scoured the Cornish sites—nothing new about library cutbacks or speculation about a spectacular lottery win—then the national and international headlines. Again, nothing big that he hadn't already gathered from TV bulletins or the ship's daily newspaper. He checked his emails, surprised to see a reply from his mother. It was unlike her to be up at this hour, but, preoccupied with disturbing memories of the past few hours, he thought little of it.

Dear Harold,

What awful news. I never dreamed things could turn out so badly for Hannah—or Chloe, for that matter.

I urge you to make sure they're okay and help them in any way you can.

Love,

Mum x

Though baffled at the calm, casual reaction to such devastating news, fatigue took over. Harold retired, giving the matter no further thought.

35

On the first of two days at sea between Messina and Gibraltar, Harold and Annette dined in the Azure Restaurant. Enjoying dessert, Harold delighted in discovering a little of the real Annette after she'd impressed everyone with her spectacular rescue. This was the first time he'd seen her softer, more relaxed side. Less businesslike.

His mobile phone sounded, signalling another text message. He'd already ignored one from his mother. Wishing to avoid interruptions during the meal, he'd switched his phone to silent. Now he took a look.

From Dorothy again, with the same message. "Urgent. Phone me."

"I'll call her after we've finished here."

"Sure it can wait?"

Enjoying the occasion and emboldened by the wine, Harold nodded. "Of course it can. Besides, there's something I want to discuss with you."

"Oh?"

"I have this gem of an idea, and could do with your advice. What I have in mind could even involve you."

"I'm listening."

Harold took a deep breath, only for his phone to thwart him again.

"Best take a peek," said Annette.

He went rigid at the message. 'Look at the *Porthcoombe Gazette* website ASAP.'

He showed the text to Annette. "I must go to the cyber suite."

"We'll use my phone."

In seconds, Annette located the site, eyes widening at the main headline on the *Gazette's* home page. "Christ, no."

"What?"

"Not here. Outside, or the bar."

Declining the waiter's offer of coffee, Harold signed for the wine and meal excess and he and Annette found a bench on the deck. In contrast to the warm calm of previous evenings, a stiff breeze blew, but huddled together, neither noticed. Annette showed Harold the headline:

Exclusive: Cornish women in sea drama

Top diver foils apparent suicide bid. Dramatic pictures from *Gazette* reporter Angie Swan.

Harold gasped. Annette clicked on the full story. Accompanied by half a dozen photographs, displayed in cartoon strip style, the article documented Hannah's desperate jump and Annette's dramatic response, followed by an update on Hannah's condition and the fact she was one of a party of six women on the cruise.

Too stunned to speak, Harold looked up, staring into darkness. "*Gazette* reporter Angie Swan. So much for confidences. Did you know anything about this?"

"No. Angie never spoke to me about it."

Harold's phone throbbed again. Another text from Dorothy. 'I hope you've seen it by now. Do nothing tonight. I'm sleeping on it. Will be in touch tomorrow morning.'

Nothing could make Harold more shocked and confused than he already was. Dazed, he bid Annette good night and returned to his cabin, surprised that Sandy hadn't returned. She did a few minutes later, looking as glum as he'd ever seen. A match for his own misery. Neither seemed able nor willing to speak.

If Harold hadn't been so rattled, he might have given more thought to why Sandy's spirits were so low. He asked no questions of her, nor she of him, both climbing into bed and shunning intimacy for the first time since getting together.

36

The morning message wasn't from Dorothy via text or email, but a summons from Sandy, who addressed Harold and Angie after breakfast. "You must both come with me. Now."

"What—?"

"Sorry, Harold. You must come with me."

Sandy led a baffled Harold and white-faced Angie to Deck 11, into a part of the ship where neither had been before. Each door they passed named a gemstone—Opal, Amethyst, Moonstone—and Harold realised these were the liner's staterooms, the luxurious premium accommodation.

Sandy stopped to knock on the Pearl door. Harold didn't recognise her face, but there was something familiar about the young woman who answered. Devoid of expression, she held the door open.

Sandy gestured to Harold and Angie to follow inside. A darkened hallway led to a spacious, bright lounge, daylight flooding in through the floor-to-ceiling patio doors leading to a balcony outside. Harold and Angie's eyes shot to a writing desk, and the wheelchair angled beside it.

Angie's hand flew to her mouth, but not quick enough to prevent a shocked cry. Harold stopped dead, unable to do anything other than return the glacial glare of his mother.

37

Regally, Dorothy gestured Harold and Angie to sit. Amid a host of confused thoughts and emotions, Harold expected his mother to launch into a tirade. Instead, loaded silence was enough as she regarded him and Angie with solemn, meaningful eyes.

Harold spoke first. "What on earth are you doing here, Mum? I thought you were with—"

"Never mind all that now. You both know what this is about, so I won't waste time with preliminaries." Dorothy addressed Angie. "When we're in Gibraltar tomorrow, I want you off this ship for good."

Shocked, Harold and Angie's gabbled replies came together.

"Oh, please, no. Let me explain," Angie begged.

"You can't do that," said Harold.

"There's no bloody explaining to do and yes, I can do that."

The rare use of a curse from Dorothy shocked Harold. He and Angie made to speak again, but Dorothy threw up her hands to stop them. She turned to Sandy and the young woman.

"Leave us, please."

Angie spoke again. "I can explain—"

"There's no explaining to do. It's as plain as day you're here under false pretences. I want you off the ship, and I'll be reporting your newspaper to the Press

Complaints Commission or whatever the wretched thing's called these days."

"But I'm here in holiday time and there's not supposed to be a byline on anything I gave them."

"What difference does that make?"

"I've tried to contact my editor, but can't get a signal."

"Good for you. I'm arranging for you to be put ashore tomorrow." Dorothy turned back to thumbing through pages of the ship's information file.

Verging on tears, all Angie could manage was a shake of the head.

Slowly, assertive, Harold spoke. "You can't do that, Mum. I don't want you to and won't let you."

It was Dorothy's turn to be shaken. Her son had never spoken like that before. "What do you mean?"

"Simple. While the cruise was your idea, planned and organised by you, it went ahead with my money. Angie is my guest, not yours. You have no authority, no power to seek her removal. Besides, I want Angie to stay. She's explained to me about her job with the *Gazette* and how she—"

"You knew she was a reporter and didn't tell me?"

Angie took his hand.

"Yes. I told you in an email that all was fine, but it was a long story that could wait until we got home. You remember?"

"Oh, yes. Right." Dorothy looked more flustered and shot back on the offensive. "That changes nothing. The fact is, she got herself on this cruise under false pretences, and what's happened is journalism at its worst. I'll still report the *Gazette* and I'm going to contact that girl's editor to tell him what I think of the whole rotten business."

Seeing his mother in this agitated state and feeling Angie's hand gripping his own gave Harold confidence to take on his mother.

"Let's be clear about this. I know Angie's a reporter with the *Gazette*, and she knows I'm the lottery winner. She's assured me she will not write any story to expose me."

Dorothy wheeled herself to the balcony. "An assurance from a journalist is good enough for you, is it? Well, it isn't for me. I would like a private word with my son, please."

Angie couldn't get out fast enough, nodding to Harold's assurance about seeing her before lunch, if not before.

Dorothy was off again before Harold had a chance to sit.

"Why are you defending that girl? I thought you and Sandy had got it together?"

"This has nothing to do with Sandy. Have you thought it through? If you're convinced I'm wrong about Angie and think she's unscrupulous, then imagine the damage she could do if inclined. If we force her off the ship, she'd have nothing to lose and a great deal to gain as a journalist. She could tell her story, expose me and my fortune, you, all of us, this crazy cruise idea."

"Crazy, is it? Not crazy where you and Sandy are concerned."

Harold used both hands to calm Dorothy. "Mum, I think we've said enough, don't you? Why don't we take time out for reflection rather than doing anything in haste? If you persist in persecuting Angie, it will increase the chances of unwelcome, embarrassing publicity."

Acknowledging Harold's logic and warming to it, Dorothy's face relaxed, but she wasn't quite done. "Remember, you'll always have that threat hanging over you. For as long as Angie Swan's around, there'll be the possibility she'll expose you and make a small fortune in the process."

Harold would not allow his mother to ruffle him. "Fair point, but I think I may have found a way of dealing with that."

"Oh?"

"Not now. Stress isn't good for either of us. I think we've both had enough. Time we calmed down a bit, don't you agree?"

Harold took Dorothy's grunt as grudging agreement. "Why don't you tell me how you ended up on this cruise when you're meant to be with Aunt Linda?"

Dorothy's expression resumed its familiar stubborn features. "No, thank you. I'm exhausted. Besides, I've given Sandy carte blanche to tell you all about that along with another little secret you must know."

At Dorothy's revelation, Harold lost his poise. "Sandy was in on it all along? She knew you were on board all this time?"

"Oh, yes." Dorothy's vain attempt to hide victory didn't work.

Harold got up to leave.

Back in confident control, Dorothy spoke. "Yes, let's call it a day."

"What next?"

"Nothing. I'll think about what you've said. For now, let's go back to the way it was. Imagine I'm not here and enjoy the rest of your cruise. Email if you must, but I'd rather you didn't."

Harold left the Pearl stateroom, struggling to come to terms with the discovery of his mother on board. He wanted to comfort Angie, was anxious to hear all that Sandy had to tell him, including his mother's secret, but only after he'd challenged her on being in cahoots with Dorothy all along.

He strolled onto the deck, Sandy and Angie competing for affections in his mind. Managing a wry smile, he looked out to sea. *I thought troubles were behind me with Hannah's departure. Now, they're worse than ever.*

38

A ngie's tone was definite. I've given my notice. Emailed and accepted."

"What?"

"I'm no longer a reporter with the *Porthcoombe Gazette.*"

After lunch, Harold, Angie, and a subdued Sandy chatted over coffee.

"They let me down and I've let you down. I've let you all down."

Harold made to protest, but Angie pulled out her mobile phone to access email.

"I contacted my editor late last night when I saw the story on the website. I asked why the hell my name was there after he'd promised that anything I sent would not have a byline. He didn't reply. After I left your mum this morning, I sent another email to Noel Williams, my chief reporter. Here's what he sent back." Angie scrolled down the screen.

Thanks, Angie,

Congrats on your great photography and story, but the bad news here is that Roy's in hospital. He's had a heart attack. Seems he had an almighty row with the managing director over possible cutbacks in the editorial budget and completely lost it. He went against all medical advice to avoid stressful situations and collapsed at home that night. Word is, he should be okay, but he won't be back for a while.

As you know, Stevie takes over as acting editor in his absence and that includes accessing all Roy's emails. I've had a word with Stevie and he says he helped himself to your pictures and info that you'd sent in, but nobody said anything to him about keeping your name out of it. Sorry.

Chin up and all that. Worse things happen at sea, or, in this case, perhaps not.

Best wishes and see you again soon.

Noel

"Stevie?" Harold asked.

"Our chief sub-editor. That last bit was the final straw. Says it all. No wonder journalists have such a bad name. They'll make a joke out of anything. So cynical. Insensitive."

Harold put his arm round her, dismissing a waiter asking if they wanted drinks. Sandy turned her head away.

Angie continued. "I feel cut down the middle. First, I was proud of myself for doing what I imagine any journalist in that situation would have done—recording a real-life drama and filing the pics and info on it—but now I feel wretched."

Harold gave her a hug. "All the same, handing in your notice is a bit drastic, isn't it? You've given up your career before it's started."

"I know but, reading between the lines, I think they were happy to let me go. There's no going back now, even if I wanted to. I suppose it suits them, as part of their flaming cost-cutting."

Harold reflected, gazing out of the windows. "Yes, that seems to be the way at the moment. In local newspapers, libraries everywhere, the mantra is get more from less. Wherever possible, replace humans with machines. I may be able to do something about that. Surely, you should have given yourself more time to reflect and consider, Angie."

Angie shrugged and kissed Harold's cheek. "Thanks for your support and for defending me the way you did with your mum. You're right, I suppose I was a little hasty, but don't want to be part of that world anymore. The one thing I could do to get back into your good books, and your mother's. Maybe."

Harold gave Angie a bigger hug.

Grim-faced, Sandy got up. "I'll see you later."

Harold reached out to her, but she was too quick

"Oh, my God. Now look what we've done. I'm sorry, Harold. So sorry."

"Don't worry, she'll be fine." Harold sounded more convinced than he felt. All the same, he felt it wise to unhook himself from Angie. "Why don't we take a walk?"

"Good idea."

The couple joined several other walkers in post-lunch exercise. Harold made a conscious effort to keep his distance from Angie. He admired the way she'd handled things and found her single-minded approach oddly endearing, as well as attractive.

"I'll tell Mum what you've done and what you've said to me. If anything can make her okay again with you, that will."

"Thanks." Angie offered the warmest of smiles as they rounded the bow, bracing the colder, windier side of the ship. Here, in the shadows, they were alone, others preferring the sunny side.

Harold steered the conversation onto business. "What will you do? Workwise, I mean?"

"I like the idea of trying the photography and book business for real. And that PR idea. I may invest in a course, it's the big thing nowadays, isn't it?"

"Ah, yes, PR. You organise the course and I'll pay for it."

"Oh, but you mustn't."

"Oh, but I must. Compensation for the trauma of the last day or two and the way Mum treated you this morning."

"That's kind, Harold. You're sweet."

They paused at the stern of the ship, the faint hubbub of the swimming pool and its surrounding activity audible from the deck above. Leaning against the railings, the couple looked back over the white wake stretching from the ship towards the horizon.

Besides, I'm sure I've hinted that if you become a PR person, I could involve you in something."

"What—"

"Not now. Later. Enjoy the rest of the trip."

Harold's heart warmed at the sparkle in Angie's eyes. "Thanks, and again for supporting me this morning and for this wonderful cruise. Most of all, thanks for being you."

To Harold's shock, Angie flung her arms around him and kissed him hard.

Gasping, she pulled away. "I'm sorry. I shouldn't, but I had to."

"It's okay." Heart thudding, Harold steered Angie towards the side of the ship to resume their stroll.

Sounding like herself again, she thanked him.

Unsure what to say, Harold said nothing, shrugging his shoulders in a gesture he hoped would make light of the situation. "Let's go back inside now. If you're feeling okay, it's time I found Sandy."

"Yes, that's a good idea." For a moment, Angie couldn't hide her disappointment, but soon regained composure.

"I'll see you at dinner tonight." Harold broke away, no particular direction in mind.

"I'll look forward to that."

Harold turned to leave, aware of Angie's eyes blazing after him. He'd never had such mixed feelings.

39

Harold's ship search for Sandy resulted in failure; his worst fear confirmed when he called her from his cabin.

"What are you doing in your cabin?"

"Resting."

Unconvincing.

"Please, don't be upset. Angie's in a bad place right now and I'm trying to help her."

"Yes, but it looked more than helping, Harold. And where is this place she is now? This *bad place*."

"That's just an expression. Means she's going through a tough time."

Silence.

Harold continued. "Listen, Sandy, don't take this the wrong way, but I think it would be a good idea if we pulled back a little from each other for a short while. You must understand, I have a lot on my mind right now, what with Hannah's troubles and Angie's, plus Chloe's departure and the discovery of Mum on board. Also, I must make plans once I return home. For my future. I have to think clearly, what's called needing a bit of space."

A sharp intake of breath. "Oh, does that mean—?"

"No, no." Harold intercepted, thinking he knew what she was going to ask. "We'll all meet up for dinner tonight, and tomorrow, I'd like you to join me in Gibraltar."

"Just you and me?"

"Yes, Sandy. We'll take a cable car to the top of the Rock and have coffee admiring the fantastic view. You can tell me everything Mum wants you to tell me."

"Okay."

Harold thought he detected a note of relief, but Sandy resumed, sounding anxious. "Harold?"

"Yes?"

"We will still sleep together tonight? Yes?"

"Like I said, I need a little time alone."

Silence. Then a click.

"Sandy?"

40

Holding hands, Harold and Sandy weaved through Gibraltar's packed Main Street and onwards to the cable car. Tension lingered. Climbing to the iconic Rock's peak, Harold sensed Sandy relaxing. Leaving behind noise and crowds, the couple watched shrinking ships in the port and bay, including the *Gem of the Seas* berthed at the cruise terminal.

Along with a dozen fellow passengers, the couple took in spectacular views all around. Behind them sprawled Gibraltar, much of its development on land reclaimed over the past 30 years, and beyond that, mainland Spain. In the middle distance to the south, stood the mountains of Morocco. To the east, the vast Mediterranean, shrouded in a heat haze on this glorious morning.

On arrival at the peak, three Barbary macaques greeted the couple. Considered the Rock's top tourist attraction, the animals helped Sandy relax more as she laughed at their playful antics. Deciding there was no hurry for coffee, the couple explored the viewing area, Harold keeping the conversation light and Sandy showing no inclination to challenge him afresh on Angie. That changed when they settled down for coffee and pastries.

"So, Mum was on board all the time."

"Yes."

"And you knew all the time?"

"Yes."

"Let me guess. You reported back to her daily?"

A frown replaced the smile. "I saw her every day, yes."

Harold's frown matched. "I suppose you reported back everything that happened, every day?"

"Not everything." Sandy couldn't meet Harold's gaze.

"But she knows about us?"

"Of course."

"How much does she know? Does she know that we've been—"

"No!"

For the first time, Harold saw a flash of anger on Sandy's face.

"Okay."

Sandy lowered her head and Harold stirred his coffee, gazing at ships nudging through the Gibraltar Strait way below.

Neither spoke for several minutes, then Harold broke the silence. "I suppose you helped organise the cruise?"

"Yes, but please do not be angry with me." Meeting his eye once more, Sandy reached across to grip Harold's wrist.

"I'm not angry with you. I just want to find out what's been going on without my knowledge. I suppose you'll be telling me next that Aunt Linda's on board too?"

"No. She's not here."

"To think, I was emailing Mum all this time, believing she was on holiday with my aunt." Harold sat back and clicked his fingers. "No wonder it didn't surprise Mum when I told her about Hannah. She already knew, didn't she? After all, it must have been the talk of the ship."

"Yes."

"Think I can guess the rest."

Sandy invited him to carry on.

"Because she was in a first-class stateroom and using a different restaurant, there was next to no chance I would bump into her."

149

"That's right, and especially when you think of her disguise. Didn't you see the wig and sunglasses when you went into her room?"

"No."

Sandy flinched, relaxing, when Harold chuckled.

"And of course it would have been easy for her to organise transport to Southampton with a carer hired from another agency, someone I wouldn't recognise. That woman who was there when we went into her stateroom. A one-off."

"One-off?"

"Yes. Hired once, especially for the cruise."

"Oh. Now you have the full story.

"There are still bits that don't make sense."

"I assume you know about my lottery win, but why was Mother so keen to pack me away on a cruise—and with six women? She must have guessed that I could end up attached and leaving her."

Harold stopped and stared at Sandy, awaiting a reply. She stayed silent, head bowed.

"Sandy?"

She looked up, pursed her lips, and puffed out a breath. "There's something she has kept from you."

"Go on."

"I don't know that I can, Harold. I think it should come from your mum. She should tell you, not me."

"Sandy. Whatever it is, please, tell me. I can't wait until we get back to the ship."

"Hey! Look who it is."

Debbie's unexpected yell made Harold and Sandy jump and look up to see Debbie, Annette, and Angie heading their way.

"We've just landed. Isn't it stunning here? Mind if we join you?" Debbie said.

Before Harold or Sandy could reply, Annette spoke. "I think we've arrived at a bad moment."

"A delicate moment," Harold said.

The trio looked awkward, but Harold rescued the situation. "We're just about done here. Why don't you take our seats and we'll wander back? Ship sails again at half one, don't forget."

"Let's do that. Thanks," Debbie said.

As Harold and Sandy were about to leave, Angie called out. "Harold, can I have a word with you sometime, please?"

Harold felt Sandy stiffen beside him.

"I want to chat with you about something I mentioned earlier. Maybe we could have another deck walk this afternoon?"

"Okay."

"What was that all about?" Playful macaques no longer amused Sandy.

"I don't know. Guess I'll find out soon enough."

Sandy didn't reply. Harold tried easing her mood.

"Talking of finding things out, the cruise will be over soon and I must decide what to do with the rest of my life."

Sandy's anticipation intensified, deflating as Harold continued.

"I have the basis of a plan, and it could involve all six of us, including Hannah and Chloe. Angie already knows a bit about it. Maybe that's what she wants to talk about. Anyway, I'm going to outline it over our last dinner together. Five of us now, or maybe six if I can persuade Mum to join us."

Silence dominated as the cable car descended— panoramic views and the blazing sun counting for nothing this time. Preoccupied with respective doubts and fears, Harold and Sandy were oblivious.

After leaving the car, Harold guided Sandy up the steps leading to La Alameda Gardens. "Let's go in here."

Finding a seat in the shade of a Canary Islands dragon tree, he wasted no time in returning to his main thought. "Please, Sandy, what is this secret concerning Mum?"

Sandy took his hand. "It is difficult."

"Tell me straight."

"Straight?"

"Just say it."

As Sandy recoiled, eyes wide, Harold realised his voice had risen. He hugged her, kissed her cheek, his tone soothing as he pulled away. "I'm sorry, Sandy. Whatever it is, please, tell me."

Sandy took his hand and kissed his fingers. Harold saw tears.

"Sandy?"

"Your mother is dying."

41

S talling for time and feeling hapless, Harold would not and could not grasp the gravity of Sandy's words. "We're all dying. Sorry, but what do you mean?"

In control now, Sandy explained. "You must have noticed how she's been more tired … and different. You know, losing her temper more, saying bad words a lot?"

"Swearing. Yes."

Sandy's hand gripped Harold's, with strength he never thought possible in such delicate fingers. "She has months to live."

For several moments, silence. The news was loud and clear, but when Harold looked at Sandy, he saw flowing tears. He wanted to know much more, but concern for her took priority. He waited until she was ready to resume.

"You remember, she told you she had gone away for a short break with Aunt Linda?"

"Yes." Harold wished he didn't have to hear more.

"It wasn't true. She didn't want you to worry. She went to London to see a specialist, but nothing can be done."

"What's wrong with her?"

"You will have to ask her. She has a rare disease. A big, long name I can't remember in English."

Harold sobbed, cheeks warm, wet.

A skateboarder clattered past, prompting Harold to draw breath and reflect. "Well, that wraps up the full story, I guess."

Sandy nodded.

"I could say Mum has been in control all along. Ah, well, at least I've done as Dad instructed. I hope anyone would agree I've looked after her all these years. I've stayed by her side, but everything has to end somewhere. Up to this point, she's managed me. She came up with the cruise idea, organised it, persuaded me to get on board and coaxed me into agreeing to go with six women. She perfected everything down to the last detail of getting you and me together."

"Yes, but Harold, I saw how you spoke to her when she tried to get Angie off the ship. You are your own man, you see."

The changing expression suggested Sandy regretted steering the conversation to Angie.

"Thanks, but truth is, part of me resents what's gone on, how much is down to Mum. She's orchestrated everything."

"Not Angie. Your Mum had concerns before the cruise began."

Harold wondered why Sandy chose to upset herself with this conversation.

"I think it's time we went back to the ship."

Hand in hand, the couple said little as they meandered through crowded streets, pausing to window-shop. Leaving the crowds, they made their way along the quayside towards the gangway. Harold tensed when Sandy spoke.

"There is something that worries me, Harold."

"Go on."

"We were talking about how your mother had organised everything, including being matchmaker for you and me and how you didn't like the idea of so much being done for you."

Harold braced himself, not sure he'd like what Sandy was going to say.

"I have seen how much you like Angie and now I am afraid for something."

"What?"

"I think you will be angry with your mother, so you go with Angie because you know your mother would not have arranged that."

Sandy took her hand from Harold's and turned to face him. She looked beat. "Maybe you choose Angie because for the first time in your life, you'd be doing something on your own. I am your mother's choice and maybe a mistake for you." She turned and sprinted up the gangplank.

Harold followed, every step weighted with grief.

42

The luxury bed brought little comfort to Harold, lying eyes closed, his mind a maelstrom of thoughts and emotions. A changed life, a world falling apart. Deceived by his mother, who, for much of his life, he'd been closest to, and by Sandy, the woman he'd craved to be closest to. Let down by Angie, whom he'd trusted and who shared a mutual attraction for him, or that's what he'd believed and now, discovering Dorothy was dying of a rare disease.

If that wasn't enough, Harold also battled with the vivid memory of Hannah's suicide attempt. He never used such jargon, but now Harold knew the feeling of gutted, as if someone had gouged out his insides.

Soon, he'd have to decide. To make more life-changing choices. What to do with his money, pick a life partner, if indeed he wanted to commit to a permanent relationship. Harold longed for home, familiarity. Back to the library and his beloved books, a yearning to return to all things solid, simple. How much longer would that remain intact? The library under threat. His mother with months to live.

Nausea swept through Harold's body. Next, claustrophobia. He felt trapped in life itself, in this small, dark enclosure that was part of a bigger, confined area. Way out at sea. No space. No freedom. Trying to keep panic at bay, he kept his eyes closed, taking long, precise breaths, visualising his Cornish clifftop.

That didn't work. Images swam, echoes sounded in his head.

Your Mum is dying. She has months to live.

Opening his eyes, Harold's mind switched to the emails he'd sent to his mother. He recalled the triumph in Angie's eyes as she challenged him about being the lottery winner and her tears when he guessed she was a reporter, but not for the *Clarion*. He saw his mother's thunderous expression when he'd assured her that Angie wouldn't expose him. Yes, Cowboy Morris was right. People were often not what they seemed.

Distracting his overwrought mind with images of his favourite places back home didn't succeed. The frantic, dramatic rescue scenes following Hannah's suicide bid invaded again. Whatever Harold tried was no use. Drained, he made for the top deck, taking the lift rather than the stairs. He felt better in the open air, more inclined to do what he'd come here to do. Walk and walk and walk. Good exercise, beneficial stress relief. The ship was now well out to sea, the mighty Rock of Gibraltar receding on the horizon. Bracing air, a strong breeze accompanying brilliant sunshine. To starboard, at the southern tip of Spain, dozens of wind turbines lined the coast. To port, distant now, lay Morocco.

Another continent. Now, for me, another life.

Breathing in fresh, salty air, Harold hoped he wouldn't see anyone he knew. There were few people up this high, the atmosphere reminding him of home and his favourite trek. Before completing his first circuit of the deck, he saw the hunched-up figure of an elderly man in a camp seat looking out to sea. Hanging from the bottom of the man's trousers, lightweight metal prosthetic legs and feet. The American diner from the Ruby Restaurant.

Sensing Harold's approach, the man turned, greeting him with a warm smile. "Hello, sir. How are you doing?"

Harold replied without thinking. "Fine, thank you Well, not marvellous right now. Difficult to explain."

"Pull up a lounger. Let's talk. Guess anyone playing host to six women every night is bound to end up with a problem or two."

Harold sat down and felt a relief that all his efforts hadn't fixed.

"Name's Tyler. Yours?"

"Harold."

"That's a good name. Not one heard much these days."

"It's a family thing. Handed down from generation to generation."

"What's troubling you, Harold?"

"It's a long story. Difficult to know where to start. All a bit delicate."

Tyler stretched his hand over Harold's wrist in a reassuring grip. "Tell you what. Don't do no starting. Never mind details, just talk generalities. Besides, a man in my position gets to feel things others don't. We hear more, see more, sense more."

Harold looked down at Tyler's feet.

"Yes. Lost my legs in Nam, but that ain't stopped me. After the military, I started out with next to nothing, including my legs, then made my millions. Built up a business from scratch. Petrochemicals, Houston. Disability is no handicap. If you put your mind to things, you can do anything. Look at Roosevelt, the president in a wheelchair, or Stephen Hawking. Despite being incapable of speech or movement, that guy did amazing things."

From a dropped jaw to enquiring looks, Harold listened with intent.

"I know what you're thinking. That's all well and good, but where's it heading for me? Thing is, Harold, if these guys and me can do all this, think what you can do with what you've got. I'm guessing you ain't poor, not with six women on a luxury cruise."

Tyler winked at Harold's surprised face. "Come on, boy. I couldn't miss hearing and seeing the goings-on around that dinner table of yours. I get the feeling you have big decisions to make and I'm claiming no prizes for guessing you're feeling mighty uncomfortable about it all."

"You could say that."

"Whenever I face something big, I do a SWOT analysis. Know what that is?"

"No."

"Take four headings—strengths, weaknesses, opportunities, threats and under each heading, write down everything you can think of."

Harold looked uneasy. "Not really me."

"Not really you, huh? How about this one? Reasons to be cheerful. Write 'em all down and take a look whenever you feel the need."

Harold smiled but said nothing.

"Still need convincing? Well, I've done what I've done and got myself a new wife, a lovely lady from little old England. That's where I live now and why we're on this ship. I started again a few years ago when I married her, and I'm well past seventy. You see, it's never too late to do anything. You have your health, you're still young. Time's on your side. Can I ask how old you are?"

"Will be forty soon."

"There you have it. Life begins at forty."

"So they say."

"You have some big decisions to make. Do whatever it takes, be bold because you know something, if you don't, you'll forever wonder what might have been and that could be a darker place than where you are now."

"Thanks for that. Perhaps you're right."

"I am, son. Reckon you've heard enough, but don't let yourself down. Seize life, young man."

Harold stood, shook the man's hand, and turned to resume his exercise.

"Mom used to say two things. 'Every morning, tell yourself you're terrific. And always start with a smile on your face and your head held high.'"

"Right," Harold called over his shoulder, smile widening at the home-grown wisdom.

Heartened by Tyler's enthusiasm, and his renewed spring, Harold knew who to approach to help with his decisions.

43

Once again, Harold admired Debbie's rejuvenated looks, as his guest for the penultimate dinner in the Azure broached the topics on which he'd sought advice.

She sipped coffee and chose from the delicious array of petit fours. "For you, I know it hasn't been laughter all the way but, I want you to know, from my view, it's been a fabulous cruise and I'll be forever grateful to you. Just the tonic needed to kick-start my life again. I think your offer's a terrific idea and, in principle, I'm up for it. My parents are close by and they've always said they'll help with the kids when necessary. I'm sure I can count on them to free me up for what you have in mind. I hope so."

Shifting in his chair, Harold assumed a serious expression. "Fantastic. Now, about the other thing. Throughout the cruise, I've regarded you as the wise one. You haven't said a great deal, but when you have …"

A slight hitch of eyebrows.

"To be blunt, you've been there and back. You know what I mean."

Debbie nodded.

"I'd welcome your opinion, that's all. I thought everything was sorted, and I knew which way to go, but after all this business with Hannah, discovering Mum on board and learning that Sandy's been in cahoots with her all along—"

"And now Angie's back on the scene, so to speak."

"Yes. I admit I liked her right from the start, but Mum always suspected her motives. When Mum said she wanted Angie off the ship, I felt sorry for her. I do have strong feelings for her. I'd welcome your opinion on the whole business of a long-term relationship. Part of me isn't sure that I'd be happy living with someone for the rest of my life. I've managed without until now."

"Okay, you say you'd welcome my opinion. What you're really asking is which woman is the one for you and do you want something permanent at your stage in life, after living with your mum for so long."

"Guilty as charged."

"I'm not sure I want to play agony aunt or that I'm qualified for—"

"Oh, surely you are."

"I'd advise you to think long and hard before going down the lifetime relationship road. I've been to hell and back. Saw Dad cry when I told him that Bob and I were splitting. Seen Bob on his knees, begging me to let him stay after he thought he'd changed his mind. I've seen my children curled up and bawling at the thought of losing their dad."

Harold gestured Debbie to stop, but she insisted.

"No, you must listen. This is what can happen if all goes wrong. So many marriages these days end in divorce."

Harold half expected to see tears. Instead, he observed a woman in total control.

"I had insomnia, the agony of reliving the worst moments and wondering where it all went wrong. Losing friends too, or people you thought were friends. Never understood that one. I suppose they didn't know what to say, or didn't want to take sides and yes, before you ask, I got suicidal at times. I rang a helpline, but, for me, it was no good talking things over."

Hearing reality spelled out with such clarity left Harold regretting seeking Debbie's opinion. Her features softened.

"When I saw your ad I thought, what the hell have I got to lose? I'm ready to start a new life, although not sure about commitment. As for you, and the Angie versus Sandy thing, you must sort that out. Give it a lot of thought. Take time when you get home, rather than decide now. The heady environment of the cruise could affect your judgement.

"I suppose you have to go with your instincts. Angie's a lot younger than you, a few years younger than Sandy, and that may be a factor in years to come. I know both you and your mum had doubts about Angie's true motives. Has she been a gold-digger?"

Harold shook his head. "I don't think—"

"Oh, come on, Harold. Can you be sure of that and do you believe you'd be able to keep up with a much younger woman as you approach your fifties and beyond? From what you've said, there's a greater long-term bond between you and Sandy. You've known and been attracted to her for so long, and won over her heart by taking her back to Croatia. Okay, the two of you have had a wobble, and maybe each of you has lost a bit of trust in the other."

Harold stayed silent.

"Correct me if I'm wrong, but do you know where Angie stands with you? Does she want you? Has she ever said she loves you?"

"I don't think so."

Debbie suppressed a giggle. "You don't *think* so? Trust me, Harold, you'd remember if she had."

"Oh, I don't know. I've been drinking a lot more than usual."

"There you are. A little mystery added to the mix."

Harold thought she'd done, but Debbie leaned forward.

"You may find a different Angie once she's back on shore, away from this cruise ship environment and her present circumstances. You've known Sandy longer, and it strikes me your feelings have a more solid basis in reality. Just a thought. Before choosing, wait."

The look on Harold's face made Debbie smile.

"Hey, Harold, you don't want to go through life on a safety-first insurance basis. You don't want to hold back from doing things because they may not work out. Life is for living. Most men would give their right arm for your problem. You, with your new circumstances and two lovely women wanting to marry you." Debbie slurped coffee then pulled a face. "Yuck, it's gone cold. I've been talking too much!"

Harold leaned back in his chair. "I appreciate your time. You've given me plenty to consider. It's a tough one but, after listening to you, I know what I have to do."

44

Dear Linda,

Thank you again for coming up with the cruise idea and pushing me to go ahead, although I still don't know who Harold's going to choose. By the way, he has no reason to believe that it was anything other than my doing and this can remain our secret to my grave, which won't be long now, I reckon.

He told me tonight that when he gets back, he'll go to that clifftop place where he does all his thinking and let me know where he thinks his future lies.

I just hope he makes the right decision for lasting happiness.

Love,

Dorothy

45

With Angie beside him, Harold clicked on his press release file, opening his forthcoming announcement on the computer.

"If you're right, I doubt anyone will have ever launched a PR career so successfully." Harold's spirits were high.

"Yes. I've alerted all local and regional media. Barring anything unforeseen, both the *Cornwall Clarion* and *Porthcoombe Gazette* will make it their page one splash, and all radio and TV stations want to do extended interviews with you. This is the master release for the locals. I'll do separate versions tailored to the national press and various specialist newspapers and magazines, plus all social media outlets, of course."

"I like some quotes you've come up with and admire the way you recall events on the cruise so much better than me. Only seven months after sailing and some things you've described, I can't remember at all. You'll be the mistress of spin in Cornwall yet."

Smiling, Angie adopted a professional tone. "Let's have one last read-through before you sign it off."

Titled 'Local Library Rescued by Wealthy Benefactor' the release outlined the pioneering of a new public library concept in Porthcoombe to use as a blueprint for a multi-million pound network of similar services across Cornwall. The piece highlighted the council's decision to look at closing the library after a series of cutbacks and how an anonymous donor had come forward to prevent closure by bankrolling the new scheme.

The article heralded an ambitious back-in-time concept to focus on books, reduce computer-based facilities and services, and emphasise personal contact. Dreamt up during a cruise, where he met the nameless philanthropist, the scheme's brainchild is Mr Harold Pettigrew, 40, Porthcoombe library assistant for 20 years.

While refusing to disclose the benefactor, the release named Harold's team:

Site Finder and Projects Manager—Debbie Jones
Ongoing Legal Services—Annette Tregenza
PR and Marketing—Angie Swan
Art and Design—Hannah Duckham
Book Finder/Floral Decorations—Chloe James

"All looks good to me."

Harold leaned back to face Angie. She looked concerned.

"Are you sure we can keep our wealthy benefactor anonymous, even if the greatest investigative journalistic brains want to get on the case?"

"Sure I'm sure. Look, I've paid for the finest professional advice on this earth—the best lawyers, chartered accountants, financial advisors, tax advisors."

"Yes, but—"

"No buts, Angie. I've been through this with you. The trust's based offshore and the structure behind it so complex, multi-layered and spread across numerous countries that no one could complete the trail even if they tried."

Angie relaxed. "I hope you're right about Mr Wealthy Benefactor's funds and that there'll be enough money to meet all these commitments for who knows how long."

Harold rested in his easy chair once more. "That's the simple part. Don't forget, we're talking north of one-hundred million that with sound management and investment will keep growing, even after all expenditure. There's nothing else I want to spend the cash on. The libraries will run as long as people want them. As for me, I'll have all I could wish for in life. The best of all worlds."

46

Hundreds of spectators packed the main square in Porthcoombe among an army of reporters, photographers, and radio and TV crews, cameras and recording equipment at the ready. Harold knew the biggest draw by far was the A-list celebrity scooped for the opening ceremony, but that was perfect. His new venture would reap every benefit from resulting publicity.

Ahead of the ribbon-cutting formalities, Harold mingled in the crowd, Angie Swan, Publicity Officer, at his side.

Angie gave Harold a gentle nudge. "Come on. Time to head to the balcony."

Before Harold could follow, he felt tugging at his arm.

Turning, he saw an elderly lady. "Hello, my dear. I read about you in the newspaper. Do you remember, I'm the one who said I didn't want you to become obsolete?"

"Yes, I do."

"I won't hold you up, but wanted to tell you how grateful I am for all that you're doing. I'm very proud of you, Gerald."

"It's Har—" he began, then thought better of it, instead offering a big grin and a hug.

After a lifetime of handshakes and greetings, Harold emerged among the VIPs gathered on the decorated balcony above the library's main entrance. He sat between a row of women at the front. Angie tested the microphone, gesturing Harold to come forward. Following opening pleasantries, and an introduction to each of the women in his row, save one tall, striking brunette, Harold spoke.

"I'd like to take a moment to remember Dorothy, my late mother. It's thanks to her support that I've been able to make this project happen and I'm sorry she's no longer with us to see my effort come to fruition."

A moment's respectful hush, the audience remaining quiet in anticipation.

Harold looked out into the crowd. "I'm delighted to say there's one person here today I'd love you to meet. As you know, everything happening before you stems from my chance meeting on a cruise with a wealthy benefactor. He wishes to remain anonymous. However, someone else on that cruise, whom I became well acquainted with, sits in the audience.

A few murmurs broke the silence as Harold beckoned the tall woman to join him.

"We had an unforgettable time together and are planning another cruise together."

"On our honeymoon." To the delight of the crowd, a radiant Sandy kissed Harold.

Raising joined hands, the happy couple glowed as applause erupted into rapturous cheers.

EPILOGUE

On familiar ground, Harold picked his way up the path. It had been a while since he was here and he found the last pull hard work. Relaxing on a patch of wild clover, Harold narrowed his eyes to take in the view across the sea. Glinting in the early morning sunlight, restless water rolled below, but up here was calm, windless, broken only by the cry of seagulls tumbling on air currents over the cliff.

On the horizon, Harold spied a fishing vessel heading for Porthcoombe. To his left, on the headland above the town, he located a special area—the site of his and Sandy's new home. He was sure with her charm, humour, and steely single-mindedness, she'd be coercing the architect and builders to do as she wanted. Dorothy's bungalow, which Harold inherited on her death, had gone to Aunt Linda, a regular, welcome visitor.

Like Harold, money and marriage had brought Sandy happiness and opportunity beyond measure. Yesterday she'd announced she was expecting, suggesting if the baby were a girl, her name be Dora—the short form of Dorothy—in memory of Harold's mother.

Harold's excitement at such wonderful news had prevented restful sleep, prompting an early rise. He had a desire for his favourite, if neglected, thinking spot. So much had happened since the days when he'd sought answers following his lottery win, and he knew there were more adventures to come.

Elated at the timeless view, Harold Pettigrew's heart soared high with the birds. In silent gratitude, he knew he hadn't merely won a sweepstake. He'd won the lottery of life.

ABOUT THE AUTHOR

One Author. Two writers.

'Mel Penrose' is the pen name of former journalists Mike Truscott and Francesca Hanikova whose heartwarming, amusing storylines laced with Cornish sea air aim to appeal to a broad readership.

Following many years working in the media, including 25 years running his PR company, Cornish-born Mike wrote local history books before embracing fiction. Married with two adult daughters, Mike lives in Falmouth and, as well as writing, enjoys painting, walking, swimming, and blogging. He is a lifelong football fan and, until retirement, was PR officer for Truro City, Cornwall's premier football club.

Francesca started her career as a trainee reporter at the Falmouth Packet newspaper, under Mike's tutelage. After working on provincial papers and in local radio, she moved into PR, working in the UK and abroad. Married with five adult children, she lives near Hayle. A keen walker, cyclist and circuit-training fan, Francesca enjoys gardening, loves spaniels (having had several), and takes an active interest in environmental and health-care issues.

Mike and Francesca started collaborating in 2016 after discussing their mutual addiction to writing. Francesca persuaded Mike to dig out an unfinished draft and, during several coastal walks with springer spaniel Whisper, Mel Penrose was born. The pair have completed a second novel draft with a third in the pipeline.

www.melpenrosebooks.com

If you enjoyed *Lottery Loveboat*, the author would appreciate a quick review on Amazon, Goodreads, or your favourite book website. Reviews are vital—a few words matter.

ALSO BY WHISPER PUBLISHING

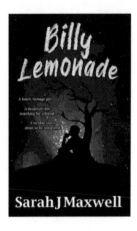

Released worldwide on 20 January 2021

***When a forlorn girl makes friends with a desperate boy,
the secrets that haunt them may tear them apart.***

Jane Smith is too lonely for words. Ignored by her grieving mother, uncaring teachers, and peers, the distraught thirteen-year-old can't find any solace after the deaths of her father and sister. Resigned to an empty, isolated existence, she can hardly believe her luck when she meets a poor, older boy happy to be her friend.

Sensing he truly identifies with her pain, Jane opens herself up to hope as their friendship deepens over drifting summer days. But, when she suspects he's hiding a terrible truth, Jane fears the skeletons in his closet will pull them both back into the dark.

Can Jane keep from returning to despair and forge a way into the light?

Billy Lemonade is a breathtaking standalone YA novel. If you like wonderfully raw characters, authentic drama, and a dash of supernatural suspense, then you'll love Sarah J Maxwell's compelling journey.

Available in paperback and Kindle formats from Amazon.

ALSO BY WHISPER PUBLISHING

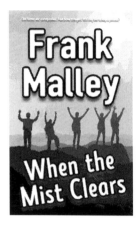

Released worldwide on 15 May 2020

One former war correspondent. Four brave strangers.
Will they live to keep a promise?

When Dan Armitage leaves his job as a war correspondent, he meets four brave strangers battling for their lives with two weapons. Hope and humour. Defiant against a life-threatening illness, the wise-cracking group quickly becomes friends, promising to meet again in a year if they're still alive.

As the friendship deepens, light-hearted shifts to sinister, when Dan's digging draws him into a criminal web and he's held captive by a murderous gang.

Can Dan's new friends save him? Will they live to keep their promise? Find out in the warmth of this feel-good story as humour and romance collide with intrigue and crime.

If you like stories bursting with remarkable characters, bags of laughter, and a splash of sweet romance, then you'll love Frank Malley's absorbing cosy mystery.

Available in paperback and Kindle formats from Amazon.

ALSO BY WHISPER PUBLISHING

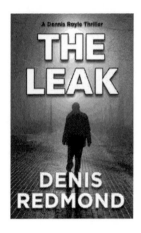

Released worldwide on 15 February 2020

An animal rights raid. Six suspicious deaths.
What is the connection?

Is a vast donation to the government from chemical giant Biomed key to six mysterious deaths?

Detectives identify a modified nerve agent. Denying involvement, Biomed's Chairman asks security consultant Dennis Royle to investigate. Amid lies and distrust, police hold the victims' families under house arrest, bringing chaos and distress.

A leaked letter to the local paper sets a junior reporter on the trail, attracting investigative journalist Julia Havers. Will she and Dennis Royle expose the truth?

Available in paperback and Kindle formats from Amazon.

Printed in Great Britain
by Amazon

66899551R00111